Tom Suddick left college to serve in Vietnam for one year, one month, one week, four days, eleven hours, and thirty-odd minutes. He did most of his time in the middle of heavy action along the DMZ, serving as radio operator, fire-team leader, squad leader, and platoon guide.

A FEW GOOD MEN

Tom Suddick

AVON
PUBLISHERS OF BARD, CAMELOT, DISCUS AND FLARE BOOKS

A FEW GOOD MEN is an original publication of Avon Books. This work has never before appeared in book form.

Portions of *A Few Good Men* originally appeared in the December, 1974 issue of *Samisdat*.

AVON BOOKS
A division of
The Hearst Corporation
1790 Broadway
New York, New York 10019

First Avon Printing, February, 1978

AVON TRADEMARK REG. U.S. PAT. OFF. AND IN
OTHER COUNTRIES, MARCA REGISTRADA, HECHO EN
U.S.A.

Printed in the U.S.A.

WFH   10   9   8   7   6   5   4   3   2

For Merritt Clifton

A FEW GOOD MEN

Contents

Out of a grave I come to tell you this,—
Out of a grave I come to quench the kiss
That flames upon your forehead with a glow . . .

—Edwin Arlington Robinson

BOOK I
The Green Bags

Caduceus

I. What a John Wayne Is

Convulsing in laughter again, I fell backward and rolled atop my bunker as Greene spilled his third cup of coffee. On the sandbag next to my head, Sutherland, the radioman, pounded with his fist, shrieking and groaning in a helpless laughing fit.

On the next bunker the rest of the squad roared and jeered at the raving Greene in the trench between us.

Greene shouted a hawser of curses and kicked the side of the trench, splattering dirt into the coffee cup (he'd cut his finger making it five minutes ago), causing us to laugh even more uncontrollably. Rummaging in his pack for more instant coffee, powdered cream, and sugar, he started over again.

We had watched this exercise in futility every evening for the past ten days. Greene's coffee-making failures were the only entertainment at Con Thien—a defensive perimeter ringed with bunkers, connected with zigzagging slit trenches—and the only source of comic relief from the irregularly intervalled shellings that forced us to spend most of our time inside our bunkers.

The number of variations for ruining coffee that Greene could perform was positively artistic—though vaudevillian. So far this evening Greene had burned his fingers with the blue polypropylene tablets used to heat C-rations, causing him to knock the water-filled cup from his makeshift stove; and he had twice kicked it over while searching for more sugar.

From the top of the opposite bunker, Jaekel crowed, wiping tears of laughter from his reddened face. "Christ, Greene, don't ever learn how to make coffee. I'd probably go as crazy as Sutherland if you did."

"Oh shit, no," piped up Kaufmann. "If you do learn, we'll have to go back to torturing rats for laughs."

Greene glared up at them, then began gazing around, as if searching for something that he absolutely knew was there.

Sutherland elbowed me. "I think it's time for your offer of help," he muttered.

I jumped down into the trench. "Want a hand, Greene?"

"Yeah—thanks, Doc. I can't find my John Wayne. It was here just a minute ago." He rifled through the pile of C-rat boxes at his feet, raising a flurry of cardboard and tin cans, jerking his head back and forth spasmodically in frantic search.

"You stuck it on your dog-tag chain," I said, hearing the others burst anew into laughter.

Abramson, the squad leader, stood up on the bunker top. "Hey, cummon, Doc. You're givin' him too much help and you're spoilin' the show."

I shrugged my shoulders and put my hands in my pockets. Greene smiled sheepishly, finding his tiny can opener, and extracted another tall, olive-drab can from the rubble at his feet. Cutting the lid open, leaving enough uncut to form a handle, and dumping the contents—a package of powdered chocolate, some crackers, and a small tin of peanut butter—he converted the can into a coffee cup.

"You'll need another stove, too," I observed, to the groans and Bronx cheers of the rest of the squad, noticing that the one he'd been using was practically filled with water, scorched cream and sugar, and half-burned but useless heat tabs.

Greene cut small holes around the bottom of a short B-2

unit can to make a stove. "Ah shit. I'm out of heat tabs."

"Here," I said, bringing out of my pocket a plastic bag of C-4 that Sutherland had torn out of a claymore mine. "This stuff works faster."

He rolled the C-4 into a ball and put it in the stove, filled the cup with water from his canteen, dropped in the instant coffee and sugar, lit the C-4, and jumped back as it flared blindingly, bringing the water to a boil almost instantly.

I smiled up at the rest of the squad. They perched, squatting on the bunker top like helmeted gargoyles, their eyes focused on the boiling brown water, widened in suspense. Anxiously, almost breathlessly, they waited for the stove to explode, or for Greene to reach for it and burn his hand again, or for him to stand and stumble again, or for the infinite number of this comedy's bizarre twists of error that would send the seething cup splattering to form another dun-colored stain at the bottom of the dry clay trench.

II. What John Wayne-ing It Is

But I noticed suddenly that Abramson's eyes widened in a different direction.

Outside the perimeter.

Then all our eyes looked overhead as we all heard the all-too-familiar—a long, hollow swathing noise like a giant band saw.

Well inside the center of the perimeter, an ARVN artillery command post built of empty shell boxes exploded into flame and splinters and screams.

We all dropped to the trench bottom and scramble-crawled to bunkers.

Inside, I saw Sutherland curling at his place in the corner of the bunker wall that faced the outside of the perimeter—he believed that fewer shells fell in that area. I preferred to stay just to the left of the bunker door, believing that to be the safest place in case of a cave-in. Sutherland and I used to debate our preferences at length, but we decided that the arguments were rather academic since, as he put it, "We can only be proven wrong one way."

The rounds came in salvos of five. "Heaviest yet," I noted to Sutherland, trying to make conversation. From many days in this bunker with him, I knew he was an excellent conversationalist under fire; and I liked talking during a barrage. Sutherland was always considerate in that he never said anything without my speaking first.

He squirmed around to face me, putting his back to the corner of the bunker, wincing and jerking with every blast outside. I could see that this barrage was inspiring him with a fascinating topic. "Doc," he began, "have you ever thought about how many ways 'John Wayne' can be used?"

The bunker jerked and shuddered like an old elevator; dust dropped through the overhead and swirled chokingly around us.

Sutherland continued. "I mean, linguistically speaking, it's almost as versatile a word as 'fuck.' "

"Sure," I grimaced. "Like, 'fuck this incoming.' "

"Right," snickered Sutherland, "or like, 'I wish those fuckers would stop their fucking firing.' "

Everything shook, and the explosions were loud enough to blot out every other sound as the Viets raked our area with their guns.

"Yeah, the motherfuckers," I screamed as the salvos passed by and walked to the middle of the perimeter again. "This is really fucked."

"Oh, what the fuck. We could go on forever," shouted Sutherland. "But I was talking about how fucked-up John Wayne is. I mean, he's a can opener, he's a method of firing a machine gun, he's a rifle sling, he describes heroic lunacy, he . . ."

A round fell very near and a couple of bags burst open, spilling their sand like toy dump trucks on the bunker floor.

"Fuck!" I shrieked.

"Fuckin-ay!" yelled Sutherland, pulling a bullet from his magazine. "Looks like we'll have to John Wayne it." He put the bullet between his teeth, bit down hard, and laughed maniacally.

III. What a Caduceus Is

"Oh yeah," Sutherland said, jerking out of his mania and taking the bullet from his mouth. "I noticed you've lost the serum albumin from your Unit One."

I lit a cigarette, looked at my medical bag in the corner, and discovered he was right; then I glanced up as I thought I heard the blasts decrease in number, giving me time to think.

Despite my knowing Sutherland, I could never get over his having half a brain. He knew just as much about medic work as any corpsman I'd ever seen. The rest of the squad thought he was insane and they didn't like him very much. But they mistook a developing intelligence for lunacy.

Even in the eyes of his seniors he was considered a trifle odd. But they couldn't deny his competence. Only a few days ago, I had heard Lieutenant Campbell, the platoon commander, describing Sutherland as one of the few men in his command worthy of that most uncommon of military distinctions: a diddly shit.

He was a radical change from the hospital school where the instructors treaded into our brains a sense of superiority to the marines. "They don't call them grunts for nothing," they used to say with smirks, as if we'd have all the superstitious respect from the grunts that a medicine man enjoys in a primitive tribe.

So when Sutherland came on knowing all that he did about my job as well as being better than professional at his own, I was always thrown for a loss. "You know too much, Sutherland," I exclaimed and ducked from another set of blasts. " 'A little learning is a dangerous thing,' and . . ."

"Yeah," he said, grinning, "live dangerously: Go to college and drop out after your third year to join the crotch."

"I'm not bullshitting. You're going to leave this place insane if you don't get killed."

"Who doesn't? Come off it, Doc. I hear this 'What's a guy like you?' line too much. Shit, it's worse than a movie. What about you? You're more educated and all that crap than anyone else here—but you'll go nuts or get zapped. You think that caduceus on your collar will protect you like some kind of medical Saint Christopher medal?"

The ARVN artillery started firing back—finally—and our own mortars began firing as well, adding dull staccato thuds to the sharp explosions.

"By the way," he coughed from another billow of dust, "I've been meaning to ask you why doctors chose that as their symbol. It's supposed to be the scepter of Mercury. What the hell does that have to do with medicine?"

I couldn't help laughing. I roared as hard as I had at Greene's incompetence with C-rats. Sutherland always brought up the weirdest topics—consistently during barrages. The day before, he had speculatively discoursed for forty-five minutes on the menstrual periods of female elephants.

But nobody before had ever bothered to ask about the caduceus—not even myself. I was caught in a three-way bind: trying to control my laughing, which was beginning to give me stomach cramps; trying to cover myself by squirming and curling closer to the bunker wall; and trying to talk to Sutherland to put my mind off the barrage.

"It's supposed to represent," I began, as the earth jumped violently and I heard an air-splitting explosion that couldn't be anything but the ARVN ammo bunker, "the 'Wings of Mercy, delivering the Staff of Life, from the Depths of Hell.'"

I heard shards of metal screaming through the air like thousands of blindly wielded scythes. "It can also represent the staff of Moses, turned to a serpent before the flight of liberty from the pharaoh."

Sutherland snickered triumphantly in his maniacal manner, sneering his words from the corner of his mouth.

"Right. Just like I thought. It means about as much as 'fuck' and 'John Wayne.' "

IV. John Wayne Cookies

The salvos became smaller: four rounds, then three, two, and finally one lone shell, knifing a long noisy arc through the air, crashing louder (it seemed) than the rest, as if trying to justify being last.

The land-line phone clacked in its box with its horrible rattle. Sutherland answered it: "Good evening, Vietnam War. Right, this is Checkmate—Abramson's got the radio in the next bunker—use your radio, he's got mine with him —because this bunker was closer, that's why."

I looked outside. In the darkness I could see only smoke, curling and swirling windlessly, filling the air with the stench of cordite and charred wood.

Moving outside, carrying my Unit One, I began to see light appearing over the top of the trench line on both sides. Outside the perimeter, over the DMZ—some two thousand meters off—Huey gun ships rocketed the Viet artillery positions while dropping flares, suspended lights that lit up the area like night baseball.

"Anybody hit?" I called, hoping not. The squad came from their bunker—first Abramson, then Greene, Kaufmann, and Jaekel.

Kaufmann shook his head. "Nah—we're okay. But the gooks sure caught the shit. Lookathat," he said, jerking his head toward where the ARVN battery used to be. It was a pile of blasted boxes, burning wood, twisted guns. The fire lit up the inside of the perimeter.

I started to climb from the trench. "Better see if . . ."

"No way, Doc," Abramson said. "I just got the word over the radio that everybody stays in the trenches, no exceptions. Seventy-five percent watch tonight."

The squad chorused a groan. Three people out of four

21

on watches all night meant sleep loss for all of us. Especially in this shorthanded squad.

I came down and squatted in the trench as Abramson went on. "And we've pulled the LP for tonight. Jaekel and Greene, you're up. Sutherland and Kaufmann had it last week. The rest of you get to your holes. Doc, you can sleep if you like."

Abramson turned to go to his hole and chuckled. "Greene, look."

We all looked to where Abramson pointed and saw Greene's coffee, standing atop its C-rat stove at the bottom of the trench—unsullied, untouched by the barrage.

"S'probably cold," muttered Jaekel.

We all anxiously watched Greene creep toward the coffee cup, stalking it like a panther. I had never seen stealth more excellently performed—Greene was almost graceful. He crouched over the coffee and took a deep breath, as if he were about to disarm a cobalt bomb.

"I'll check its heat with my finger," Greene gloated. "No, wait. It might still be too hot and it'll burn my finger and I'll knock it over." He looked back at us, smiling and seeking approval. Then he looked through his pile of rubble, producing a John Wayne cookie—a chocolate-covered hockey puck that came with three fillings: coconut, vanilla, or maple. He held it up to us and pantomimed dunking it like a doughnut.

"Brilliant," exclaimed Sutherland.

Greene dipped the John Wayne cookie into the coffee with the surehandedness of a brain surgeon. Then, scrutinizing it, he carefully extracted the half-coffee-soaked disk and brought it to his mouth as we waited watchfully.

"Not hot, but at least warm," said Greene casually, just as the coffee cup tipped, spilling onto the trench floor.

V. Youth in Asia

Deciding the bunker was too damned hot, I chose to try sleeping near Abramson's sandbagged fighting hole, knowing fully that I'd end up talking to him to help him stay awake. To ease the squad's pain from lack of sleep, Abramson himself would stay up all night. He was just that way.

We watched Jaekel and Greene crawling out of the trench and into the dark, toward the listening post past the edge of the wire, where they would fight with themselves to stay awake all night and hope that the Viets wouldn't come.

Abramson and I talked the usual shit:

"How short are you now, Doc?"

"About four more months."

And:

"When do you get out?"

"Soon as my tour's over."

"Shit. I still got two years to go."

And:

"What did you do on the outside, Abe?"

"Hung out."

An advantage of being "the Doc" was that everyone looked upon me as being different—but accepted me even though I wasn't a marine. And being different made me easy to confide in.

I listened to Abramson tell me of his trial for petty theft at age nineteen. How the judge had offered him either a year in prison or four years in the corps—with a gunnery sergeant standing beside him in dress blues.

Like a bartender, I'd heard everyone's life story at one time or another. And what occurred to me as I listened to Abramson was that he talked of his trial as if it were one of the happiest times of his life. He even laughed about it.

After a while, I found myself drifting in a half sleep that carried with it a dream of writing on paper that sometimes spoke to me, with my own voice.

"You aren't young anymore," the words with my voice said. "None of them are either—not Sutherland, not Abramson, not Jaekel, Greene, or Kaufmann. You're all old men. The movies lie; there are no young men in war. You're nineteen or twenty, and you become old with your first case of the Viet shits. "Your youth drops purgatively out your asshole during your first week in Vietnam. And you realize that from then on you're vulnerable—and you're old because of it. Being vulnerable makes you, at any second, as old as you might ever be."

"Doc," Abramson said, shaking my shoulder and waking me from the sleeping voice, "LP's got movement out there." He jerked his head toward the wire.

Sutherland popped his head out of the bunker that housed the land-line phone. "They're coming in, Abe—said they won't use a signal flare, so we better pass the word."

I heard stage whispers transferred from fighting hole to fighting hole down the line, "LP comin' in."

Then Abramson froze as we both heard the hollow, tom-tom-like beat of mortars outside the perimeter. There were no more whispers. "Incoming!" Abramson yelled.

Elongated swishes sliced over our heads, followed by dull explosions that rocked the center of the perimeter and grew louder, creeping toward our backs.

We crawled on hands and knees to the bunkers. Inside, Sutherland talked on the radio, peering out the bunker's embrasure, watching for Greene and Jaekel. "That's affirm," he drawled in the unagitated monotone peculiar to radio operators. "Lima Papa is trying to get in, but—nope, there's no show yet. Will advise when . . . Oh Jesus!" His eyes widened and I could see a flickering light on his face.

I rushed to the embrasure to look out.

Trip flares attached to the wire popped on like blinding fireflies; they lit up the front of the perimeter and billowed smoke from their burned magnesium that hovered about three feet from the ground. Below the smoke, I could see silhouettes of legs running confusedly about, frantically starting and stopping about seventy meters off.

In front of the legs, I saw Jaekel and Greene—two weird shadows like savages dancing before fire—running toward us. But a burst of automatic fire came from out of the fog—one of the shadows froze and writhed with the impact of every round, as if the bullets entering his body were all that kept him on his feet. I watched him fall, and watched the other shadow drop to a crawl, trying to drag him in.

"This is Checkmate," Sutherland yelled into his radio. "We've got heavy troop movement in front of this position —automatic weapons, satchel charges, the works."

The rounds continued to explode outside the bunker, but we wouldn't be able to remain inside any longer. Sutherland shouldered his radio, grabbed his rifle, and headed outside without a word.

I followed him and heard the rifle fire snapping and buzzing above our heads. Looking out, I saw the advancing Viets—still sixty meters or so off, not having their assault lines formed up yet—screaming and firing and throwing grenades. Our line opened fire and the Viets began dropping.

Twenty meters from the trench, I saw Jaekel and Greene. In the light of an overhead flare, I could see that it was Greene who was hit. Jaekel dragged him, not even knowing if he was still alive.

There wasn't time to think. All I remember is wrapping my Unit One around my shoulders, drawing my pistol, and crawling from the trench. I watched the assault line carefully, gambling that they'd be too tied up with the withering fire from the trenches to notice me crawling on my stomach.

I finally reached them. "Get outta here, Jaekel," I screamed over the firing and Greene's groans. "Cover us on the way in." Jaekel rolled to one side and began crawling backwards, his rifle pointed toward the advancing Viets. "Cummon, Doc!"

Greene's body was torn and battered from at least fifteen rounds—his left arm twisted behind him, attached to his shoulder by a thin shred of muscle; both his legs were shattered and jagged pieces of bone gouged through his flesh; a gaping hole the size of a football in his stomach belched forth blood until the ground beneath him was saturated. His groans became screams with every tug of my hands.

Each scream, increasing in pitch, hit me like a hammer —a judge's gavel that ruled beyond doubt that he couldn't possibly live.

I looked up to see two Viets not ten meters away—the only ones to get this close to the trenches.

From behind I heard the sharp clacking of Jaekel's rifle. I fired myself and heard the rounds thudding into their bodies, snapping their bones. Greene screamed my name and writhed in terrified pain.

And in a split second everything ran through my brain: Greene couldn't live until morning—he'd be damned lucky to live until we got back to the trench; we'd never get him to an aid station in time—no chopper would try to land at a place that was getting overrun; his sobbing screams told me how much pain he was in—but morphine would just put him to sleep, during which time he'd die; and dragging him like this was just tearing his body apart even worse than the rounds already had.

Still fifteen meters from the trench, I reloaded my pistol with another magazine and continued to crawl and drag, turning to fire at the Viet assault line and trying to deafen myself to Greene's delirious and choking screams.

Finally, I was deaf, and numb, and blind. In fact, it even felt like it was someone else who turned, put the pistol to Greene's temple, and pulled the trigger.

VI. C-Rat

Like a low-budget horror movie where the monsters only come out at night, the attack stopped when the sun rose.

But the horror lingered, hanging over Con Thien like a plague. Smoke and flames burped from bunkers that had been blown up by Viet satchel charges on the heaviest-hit side of the lines. Transformed into treaded flame, two amtracks flared and smoked, filling the air with a stench like bus exhaust.

Chunks of Viet flesh hung gorily from the barbed wire,

an outdoor butcher shop, and hundreds of Viet dead lay scattered in grotesque, armless, legless, and headless death between the wire and the trench line.

Next to the command post bunker we deposited our own dead. I carried Greene's body there myself and rolled it in a waterproof poncho. With its blasted legs sticking out like a badly dressed store mannequin, it lay among the thirty-five others waiting for the choppers that would carry them south—to be placed in green cocoonlike bags, from which they would emerge only at Graves Registration.

Our side of the lines had been the lightest hit—Greene was our only casualty. And I thought about that as I walked back to the bunkers. Nobody would ever know, except me. Could I tell anyone? Could I tell Sutherland?

I knew I'd have to sometime. "Yes," I thought, "Sutherland will understand. Who else would?" I looked for him in the bunker, but it was empty. Then I looked out toward the wire.

The squad walked along the line of Viet dead, followed by a mule—a motorized, four-wheeled flatbed cart. Abramson led them, shooting each of the bodies as his squad drew near them, in case any were still alive.

As I walked closer, I saw Sutherland, Kaufmann, and Jaekel loading the corpses onto the mule, flinging them by the arms and legs—the ones that had arms and legs—building a stack of bodies that tangled like a toy box full of discarded dolls.

They loaded the last dead Viet on the mule, and we all watched as the driver headed for the huge pit that the bulldozers were already digging. Mules from each side of the lines converged on the pit. They backed toward it until they dumped their loads and then drove off for more.

"Sutherland," I called.

He turned toward me with the dazed and exhausted eyes shown so often in photo essays on war and ran past me toward the bunker. The rest of the squad gathered around me as we watched Sutherland grab his entrenching tool and begin frantically digging a hole. His arms threshed up and down like a man mad with greed, digging for treasure,

27

until he suddenly threw the short shovel aside, dropped to his hands and knees, and vomited into the hole.

"Doc, what's the matter with Sutherland?" Abramson asked toward sunset. "I mean, is he flippin' out? I gotta know."

Sutherland had spent the last four hours sitting atop his bunker, arms wrapped around his knees, rocking back and forth, staring at the wire.

We had spent the entire day counting bodies, collecting their gear and weapons, and dumping the carcasses into the huge pit by the command-post bunker. It had gotten to Sutherland worse than it had to anyone else.

"I mean," continued Abramson, "I always thought he was a little dingy. But he's valuable—he's a damn good man."

"Let him sleep it off," I said. "He's got a case of fatigue, but he'll be okay when they pull us out."

I knew where Sutherland was—like me he had toured the lines in the early morning and had seen everything. I was there myself. I couldn't stand without dizziness, couldn't eat without gagging, couldn't think without seeing flames and blood and burning flesh—and Greene's face, just before I put the round into his brain; a face that feared death and begged for it at the same time.

Kaufmann ran up and jerked me by the arm. "Cummon, Doc—we got one." His face contorted, eyes widened with brutality. "Look," he said, pointing to the front of his bunker, where I saw Jaekel on his knees, bending toward the ground.

Drawing nearer, I saw that Jaekel bent over an anthill, where red ants ran about like a frightened mob. From the top of the anthill protruded the head of a rat, squinting from the few rays of sunlight left.

"Kaufmann," Jaekel growled, "gimme your John Wayne."

"Little fucker," he addressed the helpless rat. "Get into my bunker, eh?" Kaufmann threw him the can opener and sat atop his bunker to watch.

Jaekel took a box of C-rations and opened it, strewing the contents at his feet. With the John Wayne, he opened a small tin of grape jam and poured it over the rat's face. Then he sprinkled a package of sugar around its neck. "Ants'll just love this," he chuckled from the side of his mouth.

In spite of myself, I watched this with fascination—wishing the ants would leap immediately onto the rat's head, eat sections of its eyes, and tear its flesh. I wanted to see that rat picked clean, as if it could make up for everything.

Abramson and I moved to the top of the bunker to watch. As I leaned back, I bumped into something, and I turned to see Sutherland. He looked at me, then shifted his glance to the anthill.

The ants scurried at the base of their hill; only a few came anywhere near the rat. I jumped from the bunker top. "Jaekel, give me that B-2 unit."

I took out a John Wayne cookie, crumbled it in my hands like a cracker for soup, and sprinkled a trail from the rat to the base of the anthill.

Slowly, the ants were attracted by the cookie and they moved up the hill, gathering the crumbs as they went, until they swarmed over the rat's head.

Completely.

A Hotel on Park Place

I collected my two hundred dollars, looked up from the board, and smiled, seeing the battalion staff club was packed.

It usually was.

At least it had been ever since I'd taken over its management. Everybody knew it was the best damn club in Phu Bai—even better than the officers' club, though we'd never say so out loud.

Bluish clouds from the broad selection of cigars I now offered for sale there hung thickly in the air, puffed by the staff NCOs while they drank everything from Bud to Johnny Walker Black. Hank Williams and some other country classics drawled out of the cassette tape deck I'd gotten in trade from the Seabees for a case of Seagram's.

> Yull wawk th' flore
> Thuh way ah dew
> Yore cheatin' ha-urt
> Will tell own yew.

"Well, how 'bout it, sargemajor," I said, grinning. "You 'bout ready t' make that deal?"

"Goddammit, Villa," grumbled the battalion sergeant major. "You drive the hardest bargain I ever seen." The colored lights flashing like Christmas bulbs from behind the bar threw weird patterns across his grimacing face.

"Sheeit yeah," the gunney from Delta Company howled. "If'n the sargemajor trades you that railroad, you'll have 'em all."

I puffed on my Antonio y Vega, blowing smoke rings over the table, thinking I'd been playing with these three too long—they were starting to catch on. It'd been over a week since we'd started this game, playing regularly every night.

"But I'm offering two hundred dollars, plus Water Works. That'll give you both utilities, sargemajor. You can't beat a deal like that."

"Yeah. But that'll mean a hundred bucks every time I land on any railroad," protested the sergeant major.

"Tell you what. For you, I'll go one better. You get transportation at twenny-five percent cut—just trade me Short Line." I had to yell to be heard above the hubbub of voices and the scraping of aluminum patio chairs on the wooden floor.

"Don't do it, sargemajor," the first sergeant from Charlie Company insisted, pounding the table. "Villanueva's a hustler. He's got somethin' up his sleeve. I sweartagod, I can just feel it!"

"I dunno, Top." The sergeant major shook his head, chewing his rum-soaked crook. "I could sure use that Water Works and a cut rate. Lemme think it over summore. You got doubles, Villa. It's still your roll."

I picked up the dice and rolled them flattened between my hands, clattering them for a long time while I surveyed the club. I knew that stalling like that drove them apeshit. "Well, I can't guarantee that the offer will still stand, but . . ." I dropped the dice.

"Snake eyes and Community Chest," I called, moving my token—the top hat, I always used the top hat—to the Community Chest square on the board, pulling a card from the center. "Bad news—'Pay hospital one hundred dollars,' " I read off the card to the chuckles of the others. They liked it whenever I had to pay—it happened so rarely.

But then, everybody hates a winner, especially when they're losing.

"No sweat," I shrugged, throwing the hundred carelessly into the center of the board. "I'll get it back when I land on Free Parking next time around."

"Still your roll," mumbled the gunney. "I hope to shit you roll doubles again," he said acidly.

"Now, Gunney," I said in a soothing tone. "It's only a game; you don't have to get so nasty about it." I sipped on my tequila sunrise, flicked the ashes off my cigar, and sang along with the music.

> Ah got the hungries fer yer luv
> An' ahm waitin' in yer welfare line.

"Cummon roll, goddammit!" shouted the first sergeant. I dropped the dice. "Five, and Chance."

"Shit," whined the gunney, who had houses on Oriental, Vermont, and Connecticut Avenues.

"Lucky bastard," groaned the sergeant major.

Pulling another card from the center, I read it aloud. " 'Get out of jail free.' I'll just keep that."

The gunney grabbed the dice. "I'll tellya, Villa. Sometime you're gonna pull one o' them 'Assessed for street repairs' cards," he said, pointing his finger in my face and then at the board, "and then yer goddamn houses on Boardwalk and Park Place are gonna cost ya plenny."

He rolled the dice. "Shit." He gritted his teeth and kicked the table as he rolled six, landing on Boardwalk.

I cackled. "That'll be fourteen hundred, Gunney. Y'know, maybe that will happen." I smiled, collecting his money. "But I plan to have enough so's it won't matter."

> Ah dreamed ah wuz thare
> Iyn hill-billy hevun
> O wut a star-spangl'd naght.

Next day, I carried my black strongbox and a case of C rats out to the jeep, and headed on my usual run out to the

PX. I went out there every day, just to look at it—sort of an inspiration for the day, a promise of better things to come.

I wanted the management of that PX so bad I could taste it. It was huge—a converted warehouse, with a warehouse of its own. Inside, every conceivable piece of goods lay just waiting for a deal to be made on it. The guy who ran that PX could rake in a pile—I mean really clean up, sell half the stuff for twice the price to the gooks on the black market and pocket the profits. That PX, coupled with the rest of my holdings here, could make me a rich man. And by the time I retired from the corps, what with my pension, I'd be set for life—and only thirty-nine. How many guys can retire rich at that age?

The sun shone on the top of the PX's shiny roof, making it look like a silver palace in the middle of the shantytown of Phu Bai. It was hard for me to take my eyes off it, but I had to drop by G-5. I turned the jeep around and headed in toward the office.

As I drove up to the hut, I saw *Dai-uy* Vinh standing outside. Vinh was a gook captain we worked with on Med-Caps. He was the only gook medical officer for miles, and G-5 liked having him around. G-5's job was civil relations—that meant we had to take care of the civilians surrounding the base. And that meant working closely with any Vietnamese official, military or government.

Like Vinh.

I wondered what he was doing there. It wasn't often that he showed up at the office—he spent most of his time in the ville or at the hospital. I didn't like him very much but I had to work with him, so I treated him as well as I could.

"*Chao Dai-uy*," I greeted him, but I didn't salute. I never saluted gooks. It isn't like they're really officers. But I knew they liked it when I spoke their lingo; I didn't have time to pick much of it up, though, only what I needed to get along.

"*Chao Trung-si*," he said, nodding, but not smiling as he usually did.

Fortunately, Vinh was one of the few gooks smart enough to have learned English. So beyond our greetings, nothing else was said in Viet.

"What brings you to G-5?" I asked, turning off the jeep's engine.

"Sergeant, one entire case of morphine Syrettes was stolen from the hospital."

Vinh always came right to the point.

"Why bring this to me?" I scowled. "The G-5 office's open and . . ."

"I know the office is open, Sergeant. I've been waiting here for you in particular," he said, pointing his finger and raising his voice slightly.

Not wanting this to be overheard, I patted the passenger seat. "Vinh, why don't you climb in and we'll go for . . ."

"Captain Vinh!" he snapped. "And we are going nowhere, Sergeant. We know who stole them."

This little prick was beginning to piss me off. Now he was even pulling rank on me. But I had to stay cool; otherwise I'd throttle him right there in front of the civil relations hut. "Then I don't get it, Captain. It sounds like your problem's solved."

"The man who stole them claims that you got them for him. When he was captured, he was selling them to your Seabees! And that is not all. When we searched his belongings, we found a quantity of heroin—for which he also claimed you as his source."

"I'm sure this is just a misunderstanding, Captain." I lit a cigar and offered him one. He stood rigid, arms folded across his chest, tight-lipped and glaring.

"Your man probably got panicky when he was arrested —anyone would—and mine was the first name that popped into his head. They do see a lot of me, you know."

"Who does?" He leaned forward, narrowing his eyes.

"Why, the villagers, and the workers at the hospital— you said it was one of your men. I mean, it's my job, Captain; I am the G-5 NCO."

He smirked, thinking he'd caught me on some important

detail. "I did not say it was one of my men, Sergeant. In fact, it was an ARVN corporal—an interpreter."

I laughed easily. "That's just my point, Captain. I do work with a lot of interpreters in my job. I'm not unknown to them."

"Very well." He nodded brusquely and straightened up. "Since this matter does not seem serious enough to you, I will pursue it myself. I am opening an investigation."

I held up my hands. "Now, Captain, that just isn't true. This is a serious matter, and what's more, it's my department. We'll just go in right now and see the G-5 and get the ball rolling."

He glared again. He knew he wouldn't get far with the G-5, and I knew it, too. He whirled on his heel and marched off in the direction of the hospital.

I watched him go, thinking that he could be a problem if he started an investigation through other channels that I didn't have any control over. There were plenty of ARVN officers—high-ranking ones—who would jump at the chance to get rid of me to cut down on the competition between their concessions and mine. I knew the G-5 would never believe Vinh—I'd done him too many favors and we were pretty tight. But an investigation anywhere would be pretty messy. A lot of shit could be dredged up.

Besides, the G-5 hated trouble.

"Stupid fuckin' Thu." I spat and threw my cigar into the dirt, thinking about how I'd like to kick that little creep's ass. "How the hell did he ever get caught? It was a fool-proof distribution system I'd given him."

There was no two ways about it. I'd have to get Vinh shut up. He was just too smart.

I started the jeep and headed for the ville.

The biggest kid was cleaning up.

Stomping on two of the smaller ones, elbowing the rest aside, he grabbed the can of ham and lima beans and put it in the empty sandbag he held.

But they all got back to their feet and waited wide-eyed while I reached down into the back of the jeep, pulled another box out of the case, and threw it high into the air.

Fifteen or twenty heads craned, squinting and shielding their eyes from the sun like outfielders. They jostled one another for a better position under the falling box until it plummeted down among them. And the scramble began anew; hands clawed, elbows flew, feet kicked. They tumbled over one another like amateur acrobats, crying and grunting and raising clouds of dust.

The biggest kid came out the winner again, so I motioned him out of the crowd—I had to keep this sport fair, and he'd already claimed four of the seven rations I'd thrown to them.

Sitting him down on the passenger seat of the jeep, I threw the rest of the case to the crowd of kids.

"Con ten gi?" I asked the kid his name.

"Xuan."

"Duoc roi," I said, giving him a cigarette and telling him to find Ringo, my interpreter. *"Di di mau len."*

Shredded cardboard was all that was left of the case when the kids ran off. Xuan joined them, running toward Ringo's house.

I looked in my strongbox to see who owed me today, having already collected from the concession stands just outside the ville. It would be a slow morning—only three collections: Mai, Thuyet, and Nga.

In a few minutes I saw Ringo coming with the three girls. He knew why I was here. Ringo was one dependable gook.

He wore his blue jumpsuit and red beret—clothing that set him off from the rest of the villagers in their traditional black or their secondhand military clothing. Ringo was a real hustler; that's why I'd picked him to work for me.

I patted him on the back as he stood next to the jeep. "How much you got for me today?"

He took off his beret, twisting it in his hands, and shook his head, looking at the ground like the three girls were. "Not much today, sarge."

"Whassamatter? You aren't holdin' out are ya?" I

frowned. A stern glance could do wonders with gooks.

"No, no, sarge," he said, shaking his head excitedly. "No got much today 'cuz *Dai-uy* Vinh tell girls to come to hospital every day. He check over and find they got bad clap."

Vinh again. I'd really have to do something.

"You sure they ain't just been sittin' on it?" I pointed to the girls and glared at Ringo.

"No, no. I hear him tell girls."

"Did he say anything to you?"

"He want to know what girls do in Phu Bai. But I tell him they work as waitresses and washy girls."

"Okay," I grunted, still looking as severe as I could. "How much you got?"

"Two hundred."

That did it. Two hundred wouldn't even leave me my own commission after I paid off Ringo and the girls. And I had to pay them. I'd never get another day's work out of them if I didn't. "This time Vinh's gone too far," I thought. "He's starting to cut into my business too much for his own good."

They still stared at the ground. But I didn't want them to know this was shaking me up. I thought I'd better play it light to show them that nothing was wrong. So I started to smile, then broke into a grin and patted Ringo on the shoulder again. They all looked up with toothy smiles.

"Okay, don't worry about it. You keep the money, this time. But dammit, tell the girls to make their men use rubbers from now on. I'll bring some from the PX."

Ringo translated for me and the girls went away giggling and counting the money that Ringo gave them. I put my arm around his shoulders, and we walked laughing to the side of a hut.

Looking around to see if anyone was watching, I grabbed him by the shirtfront and slapped him across the face.

"You ever let this happen again, you little sonofabitch," I hissed through clenched teeth, "I'll beat the shit outta you!"

He nodded, eyes widened in fright. I pushed him against the side of the hut, walked to the jeep, and started it.

Casting a glance toward Ringo as I put the jeep in gear, I yelled, "Don't forget!"

I drove away, watching him in the rear-view mirror, standing in a dusty cloud.

It was just about time for chow, so I headed back to the base. The staff NCO mess was never crowded. I liked eating without crowds. It was one of the privileges of rank—plates, too, not metal trays, and small tables, not picnic-style with wooden benches.

The sergeant major waved me over to his table when he saw me come in. He was making one of his rare appearances at the mess hall. He usually had his chow brought to him at his quarters.

"How's things at the ville?" he asked, shoveling a fork full of corn into his mouth.

"Not bad, sargemajor. They seem pretty happy out there."

"Good. That's part of the job, Villa. Keep 'em happy and they'll be less prone to help Charlie."

"Thassright, sargemajor." I cut into my steak.

"Uh—I wanted to ask you," he began, looking around to see if anyone was listening in. "I'm throwing a little party for Hoffman—you know, the manager of the PX. He's rotating and I wanted to know if you could set me up with some booze. Good stuff—a variety."

I nodded, buttering my bread. "When's it set for?"

"Tomorrow night—you're invited, of course."

"Well, I'll probably be tied up at the club. Got a battalion coming in from the field that day—they'll be pretty thirsty. Maybe I can drop by later. But I'll be glad to set it up for you. A case sound all right?"

"Out*standing*."

"Any preferences?"

"J&B for Scotch, V.O. for whiskey—and can you swing for some Beefeater's? The Colonel said he might drop in, and he likes martinis."

"Consider it done, sargemajor," I said, beaming. I

thought it would be no sweat to get the stuff from that army staff who ran special services and who was always hounding me to get him laid by one of the better-looking broads in the ville. What was his name? Well, I had a file on him in my strongbox. I could check later.

"How about the price?" muttered the sergeant major.

"Forty percent off cost sound okay?"

He chuckled. "Okay? Villa, you're more reasonable in the real world than you are on the Monopoly board."

We both laughed, and he sat back in his chair, lighting a cigar. "Y'know, Villa, I think you're just the man to fill Hoffman's billet. You got a real business head."

"I do my best, sargemajor." I smiled modestly, turning on the humility that I knew superiors liked to see.

"Where'd you ever pick it up?"

"It's a long story, sargemajor." I talked between mouthfuls of steak and mashed potatoes and gulps of coffee. "I guess it was on the street. Live in East L.A., and you gotta be on the hustle all the time if you want to survive. I just decided when I was a kid that I'd be the best. You're either the best, or you're nothin'. I guess that's what brought me to the corps when I was seventeen. I just wanted to be with the best."

"Well, you got a great career ahead of you, Villa. You got the right attitude. Sounds like you've found a home in the corps," he said, smiling paternally.

"It's my life."

He got up to leave. "I'll see what I can do for you on the PX. I can't promise anything, but I do know the right people."

"Thank you, sargemajor. I'll have your case delivered tonight."

I finished my lunch and lit a cigar, musing and smiling to myself. Things were starting to look up. The sergeant major carried a lot of weight, and my chances for getting the PX were better with him on my side.

Now all I had to do was find some way of getting rid of Vinh.

Vinh. Just the thought of that little prick ruined the rest

of my happy after-lunch musings. I was really pissed. If he kept up his shit with all my broads, I'd start losing bigger money. And I'd been on the hustle too long to be slowed up by some skinny little gook smartass.

There just had to be a way.

With Vinh still on my mind, I drove out the main gate, heading toward my other concession stands to collect. Driving past an old French bunker just at the outside of the base, a familiar smell brought me out of my thoughts of Vinh.

It was just a sweet-sour whiff that I'd smelled in many a drug lecture from the higher-ups. It seemed to be coming from inside the French bunker.

I stopped the jeep and got out, creeping toward the bunker like it was a gook position. The smell grew stronger, and inside I could hear coughing and laughter.

I pulled my .45 and looked in.

Two pfc's sat smoking grass. It was perfect—I'd caught them with the goods. I smiled triumphantly to myself. Sergeant Major would really like this—be a real feather in my cap, and another reason for him to work a little harder on getting me the PX.

"Okay, marines," I growled. "Cummon out."

They tried to get rid of the joints, stamping them into the dirt floor of the bunker. "Don't bother tryin' to hide 'em," I yelled. "I saw 'em and smelled 'em. That's all it takes. Now get out here!"

Crawling from the bunker, squinting in the sunlight like moles, they stood together, weaving back and forth, white-faced and bleary-eyed. They looked really young—like they didn't have much time in.

"What's your outfit?"

"Ch-Charlie Com-Company, Sergeant," one of them stammered.

"You on post?"

"No, Sergeant."

"Skatin' a detail?"

They both nodded.

"What! I can't hear you! S'pect me to hear yer fuckin' brains rattlin'?"

"Yes, Sergeant," they both answered.

"What are you, couple of wiseasses? So you expect me to hear your brains rattle, huh?"

"I meant . . ."

"You meant? You meant? I don't give a shit what you meant, you little pukes. You're skatin' a detail and smokin' dope, an' I caught you both. You're under arrest. Get in that fuckin' jeep."

They walked ahead of me and got in the back. I smiled at how scared they were. I was right about them—just a couple of boots, probably hadn't been in the country more than two months.

It was then that the idea hit me. They'd do anything to stay out of jail if I scared them enough.

Anything.

I started the jeep and drove toward the gate thinking, "Why not?"

"You turds know who I am?"

"No, sir."

" 'Sir,' " I laughed to myself. I really had them scared shitless. But so much the better. They didn't know me. We drove through the gate, and I made a turn down the road, heading for the brig.

As it came into view, I slowed the jeep down to give them a good long look at it. Fences made of two-by-fours and barbed wire surrounded the sand compound. Two bulldog-faced MPs stood just inside the gate. In the sandy interior, prisoners did close order drill and calisthenics under an afternoon sun that had the temperature glued at ninety-eight.

I stopped the jeep and turned around in my seat to face them. "That's just the beginning," I said, jerking my thumb toward the compound. "They'll hold you there until your court-martial's over. Then they'll send you in the brig of some ship to San Diego, or Portsmouth. You've heard of those places, I guess?"

They both stared fixedly and silently at the compound.

"I can't hear you!"

"Yessir!" they answered with one voice like recruits.

"You'll get five years for sure, and a dishonorable."

One of them started to shake.

"That's five years of guards harassing you. You think boot camp was bad? You'll pray you were back in boot after you been there a week. At least in boot, they fuck with all of you if they fuck with one. But in jail, you get personal attention."

The other one hung his head, supporting it with his hands, his elbows resting on his knees.

I could see I had them both—they were beaten, resigned to the horseshit that the next five years promised to be. It was time for my ploy.

"Unless," I said, dropping it casually, "you can see your way clear to do something."

They both looked up.

"There is a way out. I don't know who you are yet—haven't written you up, and you don't know who I am, so I'll tell you.

"I work for CID," I lied, knowing that dropping the name Criminal Investigation Division would shake them up. "We could arrange to forget the whole thing—no court-martial, no jail, no dishonorable, if you'd do a job for us. No questions asked."

They looked at each other.

"Face it. It's either that or," I pointed to the compound, "this. Whaddya say?"

One more glance at the brig was enough for them to make up their minds. They both nodded.

I grinned and started the jeep, turning it around and leaving the brig behind. "Okay." I lit a cigar as I drove toward the hospital. "I'll show you the job, then drop you off where I found you."

We drove back out the gate. "Like I said, CID's my job, and we've found out that one of our most trusted Viet officers is workin' with Charlie."

Approaching the hospital, I saw a long line of civilians

queued up outside, and Vinh on the hospital steps, treating each one in turn.

"Him," I said, pointing to Vinh with my cigar. "He takes this road back to the base every night. He walks. Make it look like the gooks diddit. Don't use rifles—knives, machetes, but nothing that makes noise. Leave him somewhere near the wire. That's the job."

They stared at me with expressions of disbelief.

"Like I said, it's that or jail. If you don't want to, we can turn around right now and I'll take you straight to the brig this time. You won't get a second chance."

"But if we get caught," one of them stammered.

"Just don't. And don't try to tell anyone about this. It'll be my word against yours—and guess who they're gonna believe? If you fuck up, it's jail for sure. This is your one chance.

"One more thing. If you don't come through by tomorrow night, I'll come lookin' for you, and you'll be in jail so fast, and so far, you'll be lucky to see the light of day again. Geddit?"

They both nodded, looking at their hands.

They were a real run of luck, the perfect setup: two good marines just stupid enough to do whatever I said, yet well-trained enough to make a real mess out of Vinh. I could sit back and think about how to handle them later.

My next night at the club found me relaxing after a great day of business. My concession stands in the ville had raked in a pile from the convoys of grunts that had passed through all day. I had already doubled my investment in them, and the gooks I had running them were prosperous and happy.

Ringo had been doing his job, and the girls were turning at least ten tricks a day, judging by the take.

The army staff was more than happy to give me the sergeant major's booze for the broad I had sent to his quarters, saying she was a cleanup girl.

There had been a shortage of shoes in the village, and the gooks gladly paid top dollar for the boots I'd gotten at no more cost than a good piece for the supply officer.

The club was packed again, this time with the battalion returning from the field. The advance companies' staff were already there, drinking it up.

In the gook jail, Thu had hanged himself with his own trousers when they told him they were going to send him to the tiger cages down south, or so Ringo had said.

Things were really going my way. I was making my own luck, I thought, congratulating myself and pouring drinks for the staff at the bar. I felt so good, I decided to buy them all a round when the last of them finally dragged themselves in from the field. Sweaty, covered with dust, unshaven, and cursing up a shit storm, they burst into the club.

"This one's on the house!" I called to the club in a spirit of comradeship with all of them.

I poured a drink for one staff sergeant who really looked like he was about to crap out.

"Shit, he was really a mess," he blubbered to another staff, looking just as beat as he did.

"Who's that?" I asked him.

"Aw, we foun' a gook medical officer near the wire on the way in—Goddammit, that's the last two operations where we been the last ones in—gimme 'nother one," he said, sliding his glass toward me.

"Anyway, Christ, Charlie must've really had a grudge against this poor bastard. They cut off his head an' stuck it onna stake, an' carved the livin' shit outta him. Only way I knew he wuz a doc wuz by his collar tabs.

"Hey, make it a double this time," he drawled, downing his drink. "God*damn*, it's good t'be back. You really made some changes 'roun here, Villanueva. This club's like a real home now."

Later, at the sergeant major's party, I cleaned up again. Everything had fallen right into place. I'd even figured out a way of getting rid of those two shitbirds. All I had to do was find out who they were and plant a couple of morphine Syrettes in their gear before their next prefield inspection. And the Charlie Company first sergeant told me that they'd be going to the field in four days. Perfect.

I shook the dice and rolled. "Seven," I crowed, puffing on my cigar and moving the top hat. "Well now, lookathat. I pass right over your houses on New York Avenue, Gunney."

"Sonofabitch!" he wailed. "I never seen such luck."

The others grumbled as I collected the money from the center of the board for having landed on the Free Parking square.

The sergeant major laughed. "Villa, you're gonna make the best fuckin' PX manager we've ever had. You just got the knack in business."

"No shit, Villanueva—you got the Midas touch," the first sergeant from Charlie Company said, grinning.

"It's luck," grumbled the gunney. "Thassall, just luck."

"Well, Gunney," I puffed again on my Antonio y Vega, passing him the dice. "Some got it, some don't."

He rolled the dice and slammed his fist on the table when he landed on Park Place.

Right in front of my hotel.

If a Frog Had Wings

Three days it had been since we got the word: "There's two R&R billets open. Kaufmann and Jaekel, you're up."

Three days of boredom in Dong Ha, waiting for the orders to come through. "They sure didn't waste any time gettin' my orders sendin' me to this fuckin' place," Kaufmann growled.

Three days of living and sweltering in tent city like Kansas evangelists, while we waited to live in air-conditioned hotels. Three days of rear-area shit details: of digging holes and filling sandbags and filling holes and emptying sandbags, waiting to get drunk in bars; of setting up more green tents to sweat in, waiting to sweat on top of whores; of cleaning out shitters, waiting for the half-remembered luxury of flush toilets; of eating powdered eggs, waiting for the promise of fresh, fried eggs on thick steaks.

Three days, doing anything to kill the boredom—trying to rush the time.

"Maybe we can get Sydney," Kaufmann said, pulling the lead projectile out of a round. "That'd be real decent—round eyes, good booze, and people that talk English, not a bunch of gookemese."

I squatted, facing him, holding the frog we'd just caught outside our tent tightly in my left hand, forcing its mouth open with my right. "Dream on, Kaufmann. Billets for Australia are the first to get filled—fuckin' staff and officers get 'em. Gimme that round."

Pouring the powder from the round down the frog's throat while Kaufmann pulled the tip off another round, I moved its jaws up and down so it would swallow.

"That ain't what I heard," Kaufmann said, shaking his head. "I heard nobody gets husses on R&R spots. S'all done equal."

I poured the other round into the frog's mouth and forced it to swallow again. "When you ever known this green machine to do anythin' equal?"

"So where you wanna go, Jaekel?"

"I don't give a shit. I just want five days outta this place so I can get laid and drunk. It really don't matter where." I rolled a piece of C-rat shit paper into a thin fuse and stuck it in the frog's mouth. It squirmed and flapped its jaws and jerked its head, its eyes bulging and blinking. "Gimme a match."

Abramson came out of the tent, calling our names. "Pack your gear, if you haven't already," he said, grinning like he always did when he had good news. "Chopper'll be ready in 'bout half an hour."

Kaufmann whooped and jumped, throwing his helmet into the air. "Awwwll right! Where we goin'?"

Abramson shrugged. "I dunno. You can pick your spot when you get to Phu Bai." He went back into the tent.

"Hear that, Jaekel? We get to pick. What'd I tell ya?" he said, dancing around in a circle.

I lit a match and set the fuse burning, holding the frog until the flame burned short.

"There ain't no staff or officers going on R&R from this outfit. I already checked who's going with S-1 yesterday. That means we can still get Sydney if..."

"If," I snickered, watching the flame go into the frog's mouth. "Kaufmann, if a frog had wings..." I threw the frog into the air with all my strength, and we watched it come down and smack on the ground with a fizzling pop that exploded its belly and blew its head off, ". . . he wouldn't bump his ass."

"You ever know anybody went to Taipei?" groaned Kaufmann in his seat, throwing aside the *Playboy* he'd been looking through.

I looked out the window at the white wing with the blue PAA painted on top of it; I'd been watching the engines as the propellers spun almost invisibly ever since we'd flown out of Da Nang. I was getting pissed off at Kaufmann, and my hangover from our drunks at Phu Bai and Da Nang didn't make him any easier to take. Since we'd left Phu Bai, where we found out that Taipei was the only R&R spot left open, he'd done nothing but ask questions about the place that I couldn't answer and bitch about not getting Australia.

"No," I grunted. "But whatsit matter? The booze is still American, and the broads do their damnedest to look like roundeyes. It's all the same. Whaddya wanna do, go to museums or something?"

"Ah, shit no. I already told you. I just wanted to go someplace where people don't jabber at you in a language that sounds like monkeys, where the signs don't look like finger-painted stick figures, where the women have eyes like mine, not like a cat's. I just want to forget about gooks, that's all."

The plane was in its descent, and I could see a long, banana-shaped island, where only a few thatched huts and rice paddies surrounded a city. "All I can tell you is this: Don't talk to 'em, don't read their signs, and remember that all women—gooks or roundeyes—look the same when you turn 'em upside down. Just drink, fuck, and have a good time. It ain't like we'll be here forever."

It was early evening and the sky was a sickly gray and the air humid when the plane landed and opened its doors. Some fat asshole of a staff sergeant in khaki got on the plane, explaining where we were, what the money exchange rate was, what bars we could drink in, what hotels we could stay at, and what laws we'd be subject to, and telling us to have a good time.

The fat staff then led the twenty-five of us to a gray navy bus and talked some more while we rode to R&R headquarters in Taipei—a place called the Sea Dragon.

"The first thing you should do after checking into your hotel is get some civies," blatted the fat staff. We still had on our jungle utilities and boots. "Every hotel has a clothing store in it—but don't spend all kinds of money on clothes. A shirt and a pair of trousers should do you.

"Now, are there any questions?" he said, looking around the bus from where he stood swaying like a drunk, hanging onto the aluminum pole behind the driver, who sped through the city, missing Chinese taxicabs by inches.

"How much for a drink?" said a voice from the back of the bus.

"Fifty cents—twenty N.T. It's cheaper at the Sea Dragon, where you can spend MPC, thirty-five. If any bar charges you more, fill out a complaint chit at the Sea Dragon. You can also change your money there at any time during any day."

"How much for a broad?" asked another voice, and we all chortled.

"Six hundred N.T. for all night," the fat staff said, leering. "That's fifteen bucks for whatever you want."

The bus jerked to a stop, and we all filed into the Sea Dragon. We changed our money as fast as we could and got assigned to hotels.

Cab drivers swarmed outside the Sea Dragon, and as soon as they arrived, they picked up their fares and sped off.

"Leinko Hotel," I said to the cabby as Kaufmann and I got into the back seat. He squealed his tires and drove through the city like a maniac.

"Everybody sure is in a hurry," Kaufmann said.

"Why not? We only got five days."

The staircase to our rooms was spiral, and on the walls all the way up were painted white stallions with fat asses. Five Chinese in white short-sleeved shirts climbed the stairs with us: two bellboys who carried our AWOL bags, two waiters who handed us each a mint julep and wiped our foreheads with damp, cool cloths, and one pimp who hawked the four broads we'd passed in the lobby.

"Hey, you want rorshow? Rorshow get you good horny. You want rorshow?"

"Whaddafuck's rorshow?" I snarled at the pimp. "And who needs to get horny?"

He thought I meant yes, so he clapped his hands and the four broads started up the stairs after us.

I left Kaufmann at his room as he stepped inside, and I went next door to my own. Inside, the bellboy dropped my bag on the bed and let in a guy with a tape measure. He measured my neck, waist, and legs, then left with the bellboy.

I swallowed the rest of the mint julep, shed my utilities, and headed straight for the shower.

It hissed hot steamy needles that stabbed me all over, washing the crud of Vietnam off me—washing that shithouse down the drain.

For a while, anyway.

I stood under the steamy needles for I don't know how long, thinking to myself. "Okay. Find a bar, a good bottle of I. W. Harper, and a broad—big tits and wide hips and long legs. Get laid and drunk and blowed. Sleep in 'til fuckin' noon, then start all over again." And I laughed out loud to the shower, thinking I was free to do whatever the hell would make me feel good—for five days and four nights.

Drying off and putting on a pair of fresh skivvies, I noticed a white short-sleeved shirt and a pair of gray slacks on the bed. My boots and olive-drab utilities were gone. On top of the shirt and slacks was a white tag that had my room number and "Leinko Laundry" printed in red, and "shoes, shirt, pants" checked with a pen. I put on the clothes and dug in my AWOL bag for my dress shoes.

There was a knock at the door.

I opened it to see Kaufmann, the pimp, who'd followed

us upstairs, and the four broads. "Time for rorshow, gyrene," tittered the pimp.

"What the hell's he talkin' about, Jaekel? Says it's five bucks, whatever it is." Kaufmann spread his arms wide.

Grabbing my key, I left the room and followed them down the hall to a larger room where the pimp locked the door behind us while the broads started to strip.

"Oh, I geddit," I said to Kaufmann. "A floorshow."

"Yis, yis," said the pimp, nodding. "Rorshow."

Kaufmann and I sat down on a large couch to watch the broads undress.

One of them was medium height and skinny, with a hairdo like Jackie Kennedy's—so I decided to call her that.

Another was short with a pudgy build and a childlike face. "Shirley Temple," Kaufmann said, elbowing me and guffawing.

The other two wore identical dresses—blue imitation silk that unbuttoned in a slant across their chests, and with a slash that ran from the hem to their hips. They were built pretty much the same, nice curves and big tits. They even looked like each other, so we called them the Doublemint Twins.

When they were all four stripped, they went into their act.

One of the Doublemint Twins pulled a Popeye-style pipe from her knitting bag and put it between her legs. Supporting herself with her hands and feet, she leaned backward and blew bubbles from the pipe with her snatch. The other three moved around the room in a fandango sort of dance, skipping in front of us to shake their asses in our faces.

I lit a cigarette, and Jackie Kennedy took it from my mouth, put it in her crotch like the Doublemint Twin's Popeye pipe, and puffed smoke from the thin tuft of black hair that ran between her legs.

Not to be outdone, Shirley Temple pulled a hard-boiled egg from the Doublemint Twins' knitting bag that served as a sort of bag of tricks for the whole act, pushed it up her cunt, leaned back, and shot it some six feet across the room, where one of the Doublemint Twins caught it, and threw it back to her so she could do it again.

Kaufmann laughed and applauded. "Jezuz, Jaekel. Nobody's ever gonna believe this," he said, guzzling from a bottle of Scotch that the pimp had put beside him on the couch. "Hardly believe it myself," he wheezed, handing the bottle to me.

I drank a long draft and closed my eyes as it burned down my throat.

When I opened them again, I saw one of the Doublemint Twins helping Shirley Temple strap on a dildo.

Shirley Temple chased a laughing Jackie Kennedy around the room, with the dildo wagging back and forth like a metronome, until she caught her and wrestled her to the floor, where she turned her over and started fucking her from behind.

The Doublemint Twins brought out two small whips from their inexhaustible bag and began to beat—softly— the couple screwing on the floor.

I decided I'd had enough—at least it was free. I wanted to get drunk and find my own woman, not have one brought to me with a circus. Usually, I wouldn't mind that, but it wasn't what I wanted just then. And I was here to get what I wanted.

The pimp bowed, and the broads scowled as I got up to leave. Kaufmann was already drunk and enjoying himself. "S'matter Jaekel?"

"Nothin'," I said, shaking my head. "I just wanna find a bar."

I left and closed the door, hearing the pimp lock it again, and Kaufmann's applause, cheering the act on.

After about seven drinks, I decided she looked like Natalie Wood. But I kept staring at her to make sure, so I wouldn't wake up in the morning with Ma Kettle.

Every time I lit a cigarette, hers or mine, I held the lighter in front of her face much longer than I had to so I could see her in the dimly lit corner of the bar where our table was.

No. It wasn't the booze—she really did look good. Stacked and long-legged for a gook, with eyes more almond-shaped than slanted, she must be Eurasian or something, I thought.

"You here all 'lone?" asked Natalie Wood—I never did get her real name—speaking the second English phrase she'd been able to come up with all night. Her first one had been "Whass you name?" and when I told her, she pronounced it like "Joker."

"Yuh," I said, nodding, and ordered another drink.

"You got no boddies here, Joker?" she said, pouting.

"Well, Kaufmann's here wimme," I slurped from inside the glass. "But he's more innersted in stayin' at th' hotel an' watchin' Shirley Temple shoot eggs out 'er cunt."

She screwed up her face in a confused frown. "You talk funny, Joker."

I could feel myself getting drunker than I'd been in months. And so I started talking more, knowing that Natalie Wood couldn't understand a goddamned word I said but not really giving a shit. "Yeh, I s'pose it does soun' funny," I laughed with her, finding it strange that a gook would tell me I talked funny. "Even soun's funny t' me. Kaufmann's a really strange dude.

"Know wha' his probum is?" I asked her and swallowed half my drink. She just nodded and smiled like an airline stewardess. "He's a born follwer, thasswhat. He'll do whatever I do, like LaurelnHardy."

I finished the drink and decided I'd better get back to the hotel or I'd be too drunk to get laid. "You wanna go home wimme?"

She didn't have any trouble understanding that—she probably heard it every night. Standing up and smoothing out her black dress over her hips, she swayed over to the bartender, who came back giggling and chattering with her in Chinese. He carried a piece of paper and a pen in his hand.

He grinned and put his hands in his pockets while I looked over the contract he'd put on the table. I lit my lighter, searching among the rat's nest of Chinese on the page for the English translation. Even when I found it, I couldn't make any sense out of it—something about not using "hired entertainment hostesses" as prostitutes, when everybody knew damned well that's what they were for.

At the top of the page in the box marked "hostess" was a number. And at the bottom was the line I was supposed to sign on and date.

The bartender, I could tell, was impatient for my signature and his six hundred N.T.—he jingled the change and keys in his gray trouser pockets.

So I gave him both, and left the bar with Natalie Wood, or 207391, or whatever the hell her name was.

The next four days were reruns of the first. R&R was just another kind of routine—a break from the routine of the war. Every morning the Doublemint Twins cleaned my room and changed the sheets and towels. Every morning Jackie Kennedy brought me my steak and eggs at the hotel coffee shop. Every morning I saw Shirley Temple washing utilities at the hotel laundry. Every morning the pimp waved and grinned at me from behind the desk in the lobby.

Every evening I drank at a bar that looked the same as the one the night before. Every evening, after about eight I. W. Harper's and water, I signed another contract and went back to the hotel with another number.

I didn't see Kaufmann at all during the rest of the four days; couldn't really say I missed him. I was sure he was getting his rocks off in whatever way he wanted. I even thought it might be doing him some good, being left on his own to find his way of having a good time.

At least, I didn't see him until a few hours before we had to leave. At five-thirty in the morning.

I lay in bed next to a number who didn't look like anyone special, after getting some of the best head I'd ever had.

The walls in the hotel were thin enough to carry any sound, and I could hear muffled cries coming from the next room.

Kaufmann's room.

They weren't the cries of a woman getting laid—not even a superpro of a whore could make cries like that, even if she were doing her damnedest to fake pleasure for her john. And even then, they sure as hell wouldn't be muffled.

Someone bumped into a dresser or something, crashing it against the wall—and then there was another muffled cry.

The number in my bed shook my shoulder and grabbed at me with widened eyes and an expression of fear, pointing to the wall.

I got out of bed, deciding to see what the hell Kaufmann was up to—not that I really gave a shit, but the number would give me no peace until I found out, and I wanted sleep. So I put on my slacks and headed for his room.

The door was locked, so I pounded on it and called his name. I saw the number coming out of my room, wrapped in a sheet, and I motioned her back inside.

"Jaekel?" Kaufmann slurred from behind the door. "Izzat you?"

"Yeah. Lemme in. What's goin' on?"

The door opened and I just about shit.

I recognized Natalie Wood, tied by the wrists to the dresser, gagged and nude, facing the mirror. Her ankles were tied to the bed that Kaufmann must have dragged into position. An empty I. W. Harper bottle stuck out of her ass, shoved in so that the neck was invisible. She groaned and writhed.

Kaufmann drank from another bottle. "Heeyy, Jaekel," he said, slapping me on the shoulder. "Haven't seenya roun'! I was jus' about t' come an' getcha t' join th' party. Where's yer cunt?"

I closed the door fast, in case anybody came by.

"Recognize her frien'? She looked so good t' me when I saw her wid you that firs' night, I thought I'd tryer out m'self." He walked over to her and patted her on the ass and wiggled the bottle around.

"Get that bottle out of her ferchrissakes!"

"S'matter. You ain't jealous are ya?"

I pulled the empty bottle out of her and started to untie her feet. Kaufmann sat on the bed and cackled. "Shit, Jaekel. Never thought I'd see th' day you'd get soft over a gook whore."

I whirled and grabbed him by the shirt front. "You outta your mind?" I hissed in his face, shaking him. "You could get locked up if . . ."

"If, if, if," he spat, "if a frog had wings, he wouldn' bump . . ."

"Look, you stupid shit. You can't get away with this here. This ain't the Nam!"

"Whaddafuck diffrence make? They're all gooks. An' I thought you wanna hava good time," he said, falling back on the bed, babbling, delirious. "Shit. Gooks everwhere I go—ain' no scapin' 'em—alloveraplace—skinny an' slanny-eyed an' . . ."

He passed out.

Untying the girl, I sat her on the bed and handed her her clothes. I rolled Kaufmann onto the floor and rifled his pockets for his wallet while she dressed, shaking with sobs. I pulled the rest of Kaufmann's N.T. from his wallet—there was over a thousand, roughly thirty bucks. And I held it out to her as she stood up to leave. I put my finger to my lips as I handed her the money, hoping she'd get my meaning.

She stopped crying.

She looked at the money, then at me; she nodded, took the money, and walked quietly out of the room.

The chopper dropped us at the loading zone in Dong Ha and flew away again, leaving us in a storm of hot dust and gravel and dead weeds.

We walked down the hill, following the road that would lead us back to the outfit's tents.

"I'm still pissed off about that cunt rolling me," snarled Kaufmann. "S'the only shitty thing that happened the whole five days."

I didn't tell him that I'd taken the money to shut the broad up. He'd been drunk enough not to remember anything. And now that we were back in the Nam, I didn't think it would make a shit of difference if he did remember.

Back at tent city, the outfit was as busy as a six-alarm fire. Sweating green apes of marines carried cases of C-rats, cans of ammo, crates of grenades, while others sat outside the tents, cleaning their rifles, sharpening knives, checking radios.

"You're just in time," grumbled Abramson as we walked sweating into the tent that smelled like a surplus store. "Pack your field gear. We've been ordered up to Con Thien 'cuz the fuckin' ARVN got overrun. You can tell us all about your good times while we're in the field."

Kaufmann groaned and threw his AWOL bag down on a cot. He started throwing his field pack together.

I went outside and pulled C-rats out of the case at the entrance to the tent.

"Goddammit, Jaekel," bitched Kaufmann from inside the tent, "I told you we shudda stalled at Phu Bai. We wouldn't've been back 'til tomorrow if..."

"Kaufmann," I yelled back at him, "what'd I tell you about 'if'?"

It Was a Great Fight, Ma

I. Newguy

Nobody ever looked less like the ideal marine officer than Lieutenant Campbell.

With his shaven head that showed a slight tinge of having once been colored like a carrot and a fatigue hat that was too big for him, he looked more like a Parris Island recruit than a "Leader of men," as the recruiting posters hailed marines.

His round, sunburned, baby face, pink like a baby's ass, was inlaid with glasses that didn't seem to do anything to enhance his vision—they looked like two window panes—and they were those gray-framed, military-issue glasses that could make even the most fighter-faced gunnery sergeant look like a twelve-year-old.

But he was my platoon commander. If he never matched any preconceived images of mine, or the Marine Corps', he was still the man whose orders I would be bound to follow.

He sat on the stoop in front of the officers' quarters in our company area at Phu Bai, scribbling on a clipboard. Everything seemed to have an orange tint from the sunset, which made the screened plywood and corrugated aluminum huts look like boxcars and made Lieutenant Campbell look like a goldfish.

He looked up from his clipboard as I approached, rifling him one of my starchiest salutes.

"You must be the newguy," he said, returning my salute, still seated on the stoop.

That word again—"newguy." It was almost worse than anything the drill instructors called us in boot camp. "Newguy," with the emphasis on "new," making it sound like one word. I hadn't been called anything else for the last two days, ever since my assignment to the unit.

"Newguy—some dumbass boot, fresh from the States who doesn't know shit and will get at least four of us killed before he catches on," was what the word said to me.

"Newguy—a gung-ho asshole, just itchin' to get into action.

"Newguy—probably wipes an envelope on his muddy boots, cuts himself, and smears the blood on the page before he sends the letter home.

"Newguy—what's his name? Shit, I dunno. He's just the newguy."

I wondered when I would lose the title and all it implied.

"Yessir. Lance Corporal Barstow. I was told we were supposed to have a meeting here."

The lieutenant nodded. "You're ten minutes early. Siddown—we can wait for the rest. Hear you're a radio-man."

"Yessir." I was glad he at least knew that. "That's what I did at Lejeune, mostly."

"What outfit?"

"One-Six, sir."

"Good—we need somebody with grunt experience. Our last radioman got rotated ten days ago. Damn good man. And we're short-handed as it is. We really haven't got a platoon—more like an oversized squad."

"I'll do my best, sir."

"Good." He had an odd way of saying "good." Sounded more like "gid."

"You know how to work shackles?"

"Yessir."

"Gid—here's ours for this operation." He handed me a

sheet of paper with a list of ten phrases on it—all ten-letter phrases like "VODKA LUNCH," "QUEBEC LADY," and "TIGERS FUCK."

Each letter represented a number from one to ten. When speaking numbers over a radio, I would have to announce what shackle I was using, then give the letters from the phrase in place of numbers.

"Okay—how would you ask for eighteen cases of grenades and four cases of C-rats using shackle one?" he asked, pointing to VODKA LUNCH with his pen like a schoolmaster.

This was a test.

"I'd say, 'Using code one, request Victor November cases of Mike 26s and Kilo cases of Charlie rats.'"

"Gid—looks like you'll work out," he said, nodding and then looking up to see two men approaching.

They saluted and sat on the ground cross-legged. The lieutenant introduced them. "Lance Corporal Abramson..."

Abramson was tall and thin and dark. His black hair was slicked straight back like he'd just come from the showers. His eyebrows were thick like two caterpillars, and his eyes were the color of eightballs.

"...and Doc Brooke."

The doc was gaunt and thinner than Abramson, and taller. He smoked Salems, chain-smoked them, and he winced when doors slammed. He had a hawkish nose, a face that looked like it had never seen a razor, and eyes that sank deep into his head, as if he were peering out from the concealment of his own body.

"Gentlemen," the lieutenant said, putting his hand on my shoulder, "this is the newguy who's replacing Sutherland. Lance Corporal—what's your name again?"

II. Free Mail and Philly Dog

After the meeting, I went back to my hut, full of information. I'd be operating at a frequency of 59.5, so I set my radio. We'd each be carrying three rations in our field-marching packs, so I arranged my gear to make room. We'd be operating at the DMZ, or the Z, as the lieutenant had· called it, and the choppers would pick us up at 0830.

The rest of the platoon was over in Abramson's hut getting the word, so I had the hut to myself. I sat on my cot and pulled some letter-writing paper from my pack.

I had promised mom that I'd write every chance I got. What with me in Vietnam and Michael at Pendleton, she'd want to hear from both of us often; with both sons in the corps, and nobody in the house since dad died, I knew she'd be lonely.

But I sat there with the pad on my knee, thinking about what to write. I got as far as the date and "Dear Mom" before I started doodling on the page, running the last two days over in my head, trying to pull something out of that blur of activity to write home about.

But what's to tell? I asked, almost aloud, grateful that nobody could hear me, my mind awhirl with new faces, places, names, sounds, and sights. I mumbled to myself.

Should I tell her about the flight over on that huge Braniff jet—how we flew from darkness into daylight and back into darkness again? How the stewardesses kept appearing hourly in different and variously colored outfits, and how the planeload of marines sat and hoped for just a split-second glimpse of thigh or panties or bra straps? Or how the untouchable stewardesses, without one hair or one article of clothing out of place, chirped smilingly at us when we landed in Da Nang—"We ask that you remain seated until given instructions to deplane. We wish you good luck, and we'll be back in a year to take you home" —and how everyone cheered at the word "home"?

Should I tell her about the staff sergeant who appeared out of the jet noises outside the plane as if he'd been blown in by a storm, blaring, "You are at Da Nang Airbase in the Republic of South Vietnam," like we didn't know where we were? Or the line of tracers I saw when I got off the plane, streaming upward into the darkness like a string of party lights; or the sound of machine-gun fire that accompanied them?

Maybe I should tell her about the chopper flight from Da Nang, over the checkerboard of rice paddies and dry fields and tree lines. Or about the truck ride through the villes that smelled of charcoal and dead fish, where the kids begged for cigarettes and cursed us like drill instructors. Or the humidity in the mornings that pasted our clothes to our skins with our own sweat, or the heat at midday that dried them to something resembling parchment. Or the rain that flooded the afternoon in sheets so thick it nearly displaced the breathable air, falling so hard that it actually stung, turning the otherwise powdery dust to oozy mud that smelled of oil and shit.

No. None of that would do. She'd have never understood any of that—and it wouldn't have eased her worrying any. So I wrote a short note, saying I was okay, that I was in the rear where there was no action, that the food was good, and that there was nothing to worry about.

The rest of the platoon started coming back after their meeting.

Their boots scraped grittily on the plywood floor, and the door spring grated and whined like a bad Jew's harp as they swung the door wider, filing into the hut.

I folded the letter into an envelope and sealed it just as a huge weight dropped like a seabag onto the cot next to mine.

"Writin' home, Newguy?" drawled the seabag. He was bald and around six-feet-three and built like a linebacker; his eyes were narrow slits like Henry VIII's, and he snarled even when he smiled.

"Yes. Where's the mailbox?—and do you have a stamp I could buy?" I asked hesitantly, trying to humor him so he wouldn't tear off my head.

In another hut, I could hear singing, like revival-meeting harmonics.

So teach me . . .
Teach me . . .
Teach me . . .
Teach me hodda Philly Dog . . .

It always happened just after dark. The black guys in the company would get together and jam—just sit for hours singing soul sounds. They had a bass, a baritone, and a tenor lead, plus a chorus to back them up. And they were good, just singing together like that.

Teach me hodda Philly Dog . . .

The seabag guffawed. "Hey Kaufmann," he yelled at the short, freckle-faced pfc with brown curls, "hear this? New-guy wants a stamp."

Teach me hodda Philly Dog . . .

"Well," quacked Kaufmann, "if you put your letter on the deck, Jaekel'll be glad to stamp it for ya." The hut burst into laughter.

Teach me hodda Philly Dog . . .

"Box's over at the company office," Jaekel said, scowling, finally giving up on the game. "And we get free mail here. Didn't they tell you that back in the world?"
I shook my head as I left the hut, walking toward the company office. I couldn't remember whether or not I had been told about free mail, and I didn't know if I could believe Jaekel.
But I wrote "free" on the envelope where the stamp should've been and dropped it into the mailbox—wishing that I had had more time in the Nam, wishing that I'd been here a few months already, wishing I'd been in combat with the rest of them so they'd look upon me as one of them. Or at least accept me without all the harassment.

Teach me hodda Philly Dog.

III. TIGERS FUCK and Monster's Breakfast

On the airfield we waited in ranks—standing, squatting, and sitting amid a clutter of rifles, packs, and equipment. The morning was already threatening us with an oven by midafternoon.

The choppers were late, so we kept to our groups as though waiting for inspection—sweltering clumps of olive drab on an asphalt runway.

I didn't talk to anyone, not even the lieutenant. I just sat, with my radio on my back forming a sort of chair with my pack. The handset was always close to my ear, fastened to one of my helmet straps with a piece of C-rat wire twisted into a hook. I could hear everything that went on.

The advantage of being a radioman is that you're always the first one in the platoon to know what's going on; you know the straight scoop from the scuttlebutt; you have an ear to the higher-ups at all times; you know what everyone is doing.

So I sat and listened to the day's action. I could tell that third platoon had a new radioman—with less experience than I had. The way he used the radio made it clear that he didn't know what he was doing.

"DEL-TUH, DEL-TUH," the voice blurted deliberately with a drawl that spoke of Alabama and humidity and depressing Spanish moss. "THYIS IS DEL-TUH THREE, OVER."

"GO AHEAD, THREE."

"UH—ROGER, DEL-TUH, DEL-TUH, WANNA KNOW WHEN TH'BIRDS'LL BE HERE, OVER."

"NOT CONFIRMED AS YET, OVER."

"DEL-TUH, DEL-TUH, COULD YEW REPEAT THAT? OVER."

I waited for the ass-chewing that was sure to come from Delta. The radioman had committed one of the many cardinal sins that anyone can commit over a radio—he had said "repeat." To say "repeat" could mean a repeat firing from an artillery battery; and if you happened to be standing in the target area . . .

"DELTA THREE, WHEN WAS THE LAST TIME YOU WERE INSTRUCTED IN RADIO PROCEDURE? THE PROPER WORDING IS "SAY AGAIN." NOW IF YOU CAN'T HANDLE THAT DAMN RADIO, I'LL GET SOMEONE OUT THERE WHO CAN. DO YOU ROGER? OVER."

"ROGER, WILL-CO, OVER," drawled Delta Three, sufficiently chewed out. But Delta wasn't through with him yet.

"REQUEST SITREP. HOW MANY IN YOUR FIRST LOADING TEAM FOR THE BIRDS? USE CODE THREE, OVER."

I listened for the reply, pulling out the shackle sheet the lieutenant had given me. Code three was TIGERS FUCK. The radioman for Delta Three was silent, working out the answer.

"DEL-TUH, DEL-TUH," he said, coming on finally. "UH—USING CODE THREE, OUR FIRST LOADING TEAM FOR THE BIRDS HAS . . . TIGERS FUCK, OVER AND OUT."

Choppers shaped like dark green locusts landed in pairs and opened their rear hatches like lower jaws. With their circular exhaust ports like empty eyes above the loading ramps, they appeared to be flying monsters that swooped down upon us, swallowed up fourteen men at a time, and soared away with them in their bellies.

Lieutenant Campbell strode up and down in front of us screaming, "On your feet!" until his voice was obliterated by a maelstrom of noise: the rushing, whining screech of the monsters, the thwap-a-wap of their spinning wings, and the clattering of our gear as we double-timed into the monster's maw.

It breathed hotly on us with a stench of burned fuel; we were no sooner inside and seated on its steel stomach lining, than it closed its jaws and jerked us violently upward. Nobody talked, for the half-hour flight went by so fast that it felt like a jump into another dimension. It was impossible to hear anything anyway over the noise, which sounded like a loudly rumbling stomach digesting a light breakfast, as if we were so much ham and eggs.

It seemed we were no sooner in the air than the monster began its circling descent. I felt pressure on my ears, and I shook my head, opening my mouth wide like a swimmer trying to clear his ears of water. The doc tapped my shoulder, and I watched while he pinched his nose and puffed out his cheeks, pointing to me. I did the same and felt a pop in my ears as they cleared.

It was exciting somehow—my heart was pounding, and I felt supercharged with energy, as if I could run long distances at top speed or lift incredible weights. My radio on my back felt light—as if it were my energy source and I were a machine, pumped full of power by that twenty-five-pound pack on my back.

I looked around at the others; they were staring absently at the inside of the monster's stomach while its whines decreased in pitch. The ground contact jolted us. We scrambled to our feet as the lower jaw opened again and spat us into a wet field where tall grass waved like seaweed.

I followed the lieutenant, keeping a safe distance so as not to draw fire. He dropped to one knee and motioned everyone to spread out. Then he pointed at me and beckoned me over to him.

I unhooked the handset from my helmet and he grabbed it from me. "This is Delta Two Red. We are in Lima Zulu and awaiting orders, over."

I looked up to see all the flying monsters dropping to the ground, puking their breakfasts into the wet grass, and flying off in search of other meals.

IV. Beau Geste

Walk, stop, listen, and walk again was the order of the day—and probably would be for the rest of the operation. The quiet of the demilitarized zone belied the fact that we were in a war at all. For once, the DMZ seemed to be living up to its name. Not so much as a single sniper broke up the hours of walk, stop, listen, and walk again.

All day the radio hissed and droned voices into my ear—time checks, radio checks, and situation reports.

"AH—DELTA TWO, THIS IS DELTA. REQUEST SHORT TEST COUNT FOR RADIO CHECK, OVER."

"Roger, Delta. Stand by—one, two, thu-ree, fower, fy-ive—fy-ive, fower, thu-ree, two, one. This has been a short test count. How do you hear the station? Over."

"LOUD 'N CLEAR, DELTA TWO, HOW ME? OVER."

"Loud 'n clear, Delta. Out."

The heat increased with every hour, as if it had a schedule to keep; and by noon our utilities were darkened to a forest green with our sweat. Even the sunset was unbearably hot, parboiling us inside our damp clothes like basted fish.

Along with that sickly salmon-colored sunset came the last addition to the order of the day—dig in.

We dug holes beside a wide trail that shone golden in the half moonlight—holes in the reddish clay to live in like moles for the night. We spread on burning mosquito repellent like rancid after-shave lotion, and sat while darkness and chill rewarded our hot day's labor with a wet blanket.

I occupied a hole with Lieutenant Campbell. He wanted to be near the radio in case anything happened, so we set up a radio watch. I had the first shift, the doc would have the second. It would be two hours on, four hours off, all night. The doc turned in, but the lieutenant couldn't sleep yet, so he stayed up with me.

He probably wanted to find out what his new radioman was like, since he had to depend on me for communications, so he began asking questions.

"How long were you at Lejeune?"

"Just three months, sir. It was my first duty station."

"You really picked up rank fast. You haven't been in a year yet."

"I was honor man out of boot camp—promoted to pfc. They made me lance just before I left Lejeune."

"Promotion come with your Nam orders?"

"No sir—it came before. I requested the orders."

Even in the dim light I could see him do a double take on me. "You requested transfer to this place?" His jaw hung open. "What're you bucking for?"

"Nothing, sir. I've got a kid brother in the corps—joined a couple of months after I did. He's the last in the family. My father died a few years ago, so that makes me head of the household. I figured . . ."

The radio hissed. "DELTA TWO, DELTA TWO, REQUEST SITREP, OVER."

"Roger, Delta. All secure, over."

The lieutenant shook his head and chuckled. "*Beau Geste*," he said, half-smiling.

"Sir?"

"*Beau Geste*. It's a Foreign Legion story I read as a kid. It's about a guy who carries loyalty about as far as you have—he had a brother, too. It means 'gallant gesture.' "

I didn't understand. "I don't see it as gallant, sir. It's just that I'm the oldest and . . ."

"And you thought it was your duty to protect your brother, right?"

"Well, yessir. If both of us came here and got killed, it'd be the end of our family and there'd be nobody to take care of our mother."

"You sure picked a shitty place to do it," he said bitterly with disgust in his voice.

"Sir?"

"Don't gimme that 'sir?' shit. Sure, you're a newguy, but you aren't stupid. It takes some smarts to run that radio right. In fact, what I'm gonna do is groom you to take over for me when I'm not around. I was training Sutherland to do that until he got dinged so bad they had to ship him out.

"What I mean is, if I'm tied up with something else, I'll expect you to have enough brains to bullshit over the radio

—stall Delta until I can get back. In effect, you'll be platoon commander for a while.

"But you've gotta drop this idealistic shit. It's the first thing you have to lose in the Nam. I'm firmly convinced now that it'll be the cynics who survive this war—they'll all be crazy, but they'll be alive, at least."

I never thought I'd be hearing this from an officer. I was confused—officers weren't supposed to be this open with enlisted men.

"Look," he continued, evidently noticing my confusion. "This place is a third-rate objective. Tactically, the whole thing's absurd. We move from one defensive posture to another, setting ourselves up to be attacked. We can't advance across this sillyass line we're sitting on right now. So we have to wait for them to hit us. We're only bait, to lure the gooks out in the open. Every goddamn defensive perimeter south of here—that's Con Thien, Gio Linh, and Cam Lo—exists for only one reason: to defend itself! Now doesn't that sound just a bit stupid and futile to you?"

"Yessir. But what about infiltration?"

"Right—shit, they really got to you. I suppose next you'll be telling me that 'We'll be fighting them on the Golden Gate Bridge if we don't stop them here,' " he said in a monotone John Wayne imitation. "Bullshit. We're wasting time here. I dunno, maybe I was wrong. Maybe you can't understand. My last radioman—Sutherland—he understood. He hated my guts for mistreating prisoners, but he agreed with me that this was a shitty deal."

"Then why go on, sir?"

He stopped for a moment and shook his head. "Because it's a job—it's what I do. Yours is a sense of ideal duty, mine is mercenary. It just beats the hell out of selling shoes in Phoenix. Face it, as long as you're in Vietnam, you're a mercenary; you're doing what nobody else wants to do because they don't want to dip their hands in shit. That 'God, mom, and apple pie' line doesn't cut it anymore—God's dead, mom's divorced, and apple pie comes out of a machine, wrapped in cellophane for a dime.

"I do the job because I'm here and I want to stay alive. I

had your ideals, too—but now, it's just survival until my rotation date."

He fell silent. My mind reeled at this ranting. I'd never been this close to an officer before, never talked this way with one. At Lejeune they separated themselves from us even in the field. They were always distant and mysterious. I'd always looked upon them as everything the corps stood for.

But then, Lieutenant Campbell had shattered my recruiting-poster image the first time I saw him.

It was strange, but I got the feeling that he didn't really mean all that he had said, that he was venting some kind of rage or frustration—using me as a sort of sounding board. Maybe, deep down, he really wanted to believe that he was doing the right thing, but couldn't anymore.

"What about the enemy, sir? Do you think they believe in what they're doing?"

"The enemy? I don't give a shit about them. All they are to me is someplace to throw all the shit that gets piled up on me. I mean, haven't you ever just wanted to start blowing things up, smashing people, just to get rid of some of the poison that the corps pumps you full of every day? Didn't you feel that way in boot camp? Well, that's the way it is here. That isn't a soldier out there. He's a symbol of everything that pisses me off—he's the heat, he's the rain, he's the mosquitoes and the mud; he's the lousy food, the ignorant lifers, the warm beer, and the runs. One NVA troopie, when he gets in front of me, represents all frustration. I gotta take it out on him. Or I'll go back to the world and take it all out on the first hawk I see."

"Sounds like a rather gallant gesture in itself, sir—doing a job even though you know that nobody will ever give a damn, even if you do it right," I muttered, half-trying to agree with him.

He snorted and shook his head again. "Shit. Even that's outdated—it's nineteenth century. I guess we're all a bit like you or we wouldn't be here in the first place—but now we're just a bit more hardened than you. We're all a bunch of Beaux Gestes. And we're all every bit as outdated."

V. Good Morning Vietnam

I had the last watch as well as the first; and as my radio hissed, "DELTA TWO, DELTA TWO, REVEILLE, REVEILLE, OVER," I expected to hear something else. It never occurred to me in my half stupor of sleeplessness that I wouldn't hear it in the field. I'd heard it every morning since arriving in Vietnam.

Every morning back in the rear, Armed Forces Radio would begin the day with a little tattoo on a pipe, followed by an announcer crowing, "Goooooood *Morn*ing *Viet*-nam!"

That particular early-morning announcer was singularly responsible for more screamed obscenities, more thrown boots, and more smashed transistor radios than anyone in the history of warfare—including Tokyo Rose.

But he was not there that morning. And we had nothing to bear the brunt of our rage: no scapegoat for the aches in our bodies from the night's damp chill; no whipping boy for the hundreds of mosquito bites that proved the uselessness of our repellent; no target for our exhausted frustration that made us wonder if we had slept at all. The faceless radio announcer was not there for us to curse when we really needed him.

Anyone who felt as shitty as we did and who could still enthusiastically bleat, "Goooooood *Morn*ing *Viet*-nam!" would be either a lunatic, a masochist, or the most sarcastic person who ever lived.

Instead, our day began quietly. Already I could smell the sour, sinus-searing heat tabs, cooking someone's canned ham-and-egg loaf or heating coffee.

Lieutenant Campbell was still asleep in the hole, snoring like a delinquent gravedigger. All along the trail I saw men climbing from their holes, yawning, stretching, cursing the day. Abramson moved down the line of holes, kneeling beside each one and waking whoever was still inside.

And suddenly Lieutenant Campbell sat up, squinted

from side to side with a look of thorough revulsion on his face, and uttered his first word of the day.

"Shit."

He crawled out of the ground, walked past me wordlessly over to a tree, and pissed, his body contorting and shivering as he yawned.

Coming back, buttoning up his trousers, he stood before me while I squatted on the ground brewing coffee. He coughed, and sniffed, and spoke his second word of the day.

"Shit."

"DELTA TWO, DELTA TWO," the radio crackled, as if trying to lend contrast to the lieutenant's eloquence.

I slurped at my coffee and said, "Delta Two."

"AH—WE'LL BE MOVING IN ABOUT THIRTY. REQUEST—AH—TWO RED AT CHARLIE PAPA FOR BRIEFING, OVER."

"Roger, out. Sir?" I turned to the lieutenant who sat shoveling his breakfast into his mouth with a white plastic spoon.

"Mumnph?" he grunted.

"You're wanted at the CP."

He swallowed a mouthful of mocha—a combination of instant coffee and instant chocolate—and grimaced. "Shit."

Standing up, he offered me the can with the white spoon sticking out of it. "You want some of this?"

"What is it?"

"You take your white bread, cut a hole in the top, and pour in a bit of water. Then you put in some peanut butter and jam and stir it all together while you heat it up."

I shook my head. "No thanks, sir. I don't eat breakfast."

"Just as well," he said, nodding. "Tastes terrible anyway."

He turned away, throwing his breakfast into the hole, and walked toward the CP, grumbling, "Shit."

He'd only been gone about five minutes when I saw them. They came down the trail together, talking, laughing, not noticing us at all.

They wore brown shirts with red parallelograms on the

collars and hats like Andy Capp's. One of them carried a radio—all three had rifles slung over their shoulders and held at the hip John Wayne style. All three had khaki shorts on, like little boys.

I couldn't believe they didn't see us—they just walked right toward our position. I saw the doc draw his pistol and raise it, saying, "Halt!"

" 'Halt' hell!" screamed Abramson. "Jaekel, Kaufmann!"

He didn't have to say anything more. They opened up on the gooks with automatic fire that tore the morning quiet to shreds.

The one with the radio ducked into some bushes alongside the trail while the other two quivered like rubber toys as the rounds ripped into them.

Jaekel sprayed the bushes with another automatic burst and a rifle flew out, followed by the gook with his hands up, just as Lieutenant Campbell arrived on the scene.

"Get that fuckin' radio," Abramson bellowed, and Kaufmann dragged it from the bushes while two others grabbed the gook by the shirt front and threw him toward me. I watched, almost paralyzed as the gook stumbled from their throw and collapsed at my feet.

"Knock him out," ordered the lieutenant.

I became automatic. I grabbed the gook's hair, lifting him to his knees, and slammed my fist into his face.

He shrieked, and I hit him again. He dropped to the ground crying, and I looked up to see the rest of the squad dragging the two bodies off the trail—blood and dirt mingled on their legs like a strange, coarse plant disease. The gook I'd just hit lay at my feet sobbing.

Jaekel came over and kicked him in the face.

The sobbing stopped.

"See anything else, Abe?" I heard the lieutenant saying.

"Nossir. Must be an observer team."

"Gid—let's saddle up and move out."

I put the radio on my back and grabbed my rifle, only then realizing that it had lain on the ground throughout the entire encounter with the gooks. I looked at the rumpled figure on the ground. "What about him, sir?"

"I dunno," he said, shrugging. "That's what I'm going to find out." He pulled the handset from my helmet. "This is Two Red. I got a prisoner here. What's his disposition to be? Over."

I watched the company forming up. They slung their rifles and talked among themselves about the three gooks just walking into us like that.

And from far down the column I heard a distant voice of one marine in a grim parody of the usual morning sound. "Goooooood *Morn*ing *Viet*-nam!"

"Roger, out," said the lieutenant, pulling his pistol.

He gave me back the handset, put the pistol to the gook's head, and fired.

The gook's body jerked as the side of his face came off and blended with the dirt.

The lieutenant kicked the body into a nearby hole.

"Shit."

VI. The Point

We marched at the point.

The point meant we were in front of the rest of the company. Had we been farther south, I was told, the point would really be the shits because of the booby traps.

But in the Z it meant only that we'd have to keep our eyes and ears open for ambush.

Kaufmann was the eyes of the company since he was in front of us all. Behind him were Jaekel, Abramson, and the doc. Since I had the radio, I was the company's ears. Lieutenant Campbell followed me, and the rest of the unit behind him comprised the rest of the point.

For about six hours the day was like the one before: walk, stop, listen, and walk again. The trail was well-worn, flanked by thick brush and trees that could conceal anything. Because of this, we walked quietly, threatened to silence by the presence of that thick foliage.

As we approached a shrine, the trail began to open wide. Soon we were in a clearing. Only a few tall trees stood, reaching high up and shading the ground with their thick canopy. In the center of the clearing the shrine stood— about the size of a public toilet in a park, half demolished and colored a faded pink. A dim path led up to it, over-grown with the little bit of underbrush that had managed to survive the lack of sun, proving that nobody had been there in quite some time.

We walked past it, all staring as if someone had com-manded, "Eyes, right." It was strange to see this in the middle of the jungle.

At the other side of the clearing where the brush got thicker and the trail thinned out again, I felt the lieutenant tap me on the shoulder. "I'm going to set up some mor-tars."

"I can do that over the radio, sir . . ."

"No. It would take too long. I want them set up to cover the main body's advance through that clearing. You'd have to call Delta, and that'd be time-consuming. Be back in a few—remember what we talked about last night?"

"Yessir," I said, nodding. I knew that I would be in charge; if Delta called, asking for the lieutenant, I'd have to snow them until he showed up.

"Gid. Your first job will be to think of something to tell them," he said, disappearing into a bend in the trail.

I passed the word up the line to hold it up, then got on the radio. "Delta, this is Delta Two."

"GO AHEAD, TWO."

"We have a pretty wide clearing up here. Request to hold it up while we set up some security for you to pass through."

"ROGER, TWO, WE'RE HOLDING. BUT GET EVERYBODY OUT OF THAT CLEARING, OVER."

This was a big risk. If there was nobody in the clearing, it meant that we'd be cut off from the main body, tem-porarily, until the lieutenant finished setting up the mor-tars. But I began to see his point. If we'd waited for Delta to set up the mortar coverage, we'd have at least a platoon exposed in the clearing, right in front of the shrine—and it was a known fact that ambushes happened in clearings.

I moved into the bush and sat down alongside the trail, grateful for the chance to get off my feet. Staring absently at the green that surrounded me, I thought that I'd be able to write a pretty descriptive letter to mom after this operation was over. I could leave out the contact with the gooks —it already seemed it had happened years ago anyway.

And then there was so much else I could talk about.

I could tell her about the beauty of the place: how the ground felt lush and damp and how the grass and leaves were cool on my face; or how the sun shone in gray beams through the treetops, making the moisture on the leaves glitter with different colors like prisms; or I could tell her how the heat waves rose off open fields, making them look like mirages or films shown on out-of-focus projectors that blurred the colors all together; or how the dust swirled in the evening breezes, colored by sunset like pink clouds; or how the jagged mountains looked like they were covered with Persian rugs.

I knew how she liked beautiful things—and there were hundreds of scenes in Vietnam that I could tell her about, without even mentioning the war at all.

Pops and hisses brought me out of the dream letter.

They increased in number until they became a thunder. Explosions shook the whole area to my right—where the main body of the company was.

I curled in a tight ball on the ground, pointing my rifle across the trail. The handset next to my ear was alive with voices that sounded like announcers covering some disaster.

Abramson crawled toward me. "What's happening?"

"Sounds like main body's getting . . ."

"I know that," he growled. "Any word? Where's the lieutenant?"

Mortars started falling on the main body—I could hear their repetitive crashes, but I couldn't hear our own firing back. A few machine guns were active, but the heaviest volume of fire came from the gooks.

"He's trying to check mortars—that was ten minutes ago."

"Mortars? Shit, he's right in the middle of it, and we're cut off."

I stared at him, knowing my face registered confusion. "What'll we do?"

He shook his head. "That's at least a battalion hitting us. We'll be out of the shit for a while. If they wipe out the main body, they'll come gunnin' for us."

I tried to call Delta, but the net was tied up—nobody answered.

Abramson grabbed the handset. "I can hear gunfire over this thing!" he yelled at me. "What's that mean?"

"Radioman could be pressing the key on his handset, or . . ."

"Or lyin' onnit, right?" He gave me back the handset. "Great, no comm either."

"Any station this net, any station this net!" I yelled into the handset. The firing didn't let up. "Any station this net!" I kept yelling. But no answers. "Okay—I'm gonna try and reach battalion," I said to Abramson. "They're the only ones who can tell us what to do now."

I rolled on my side and told Abramson to set the radio for the battalion frequency. "Permission, Permission, this is Delta Two. Mayday, Mayday, over."

"DELTA TWO, THIS IS PERMISSION—WHAT IS YOUR LOCATION? OVER."

Abramson pulled his map out and read our position to them.

"ROGER, DELTA TWO—AH—PROCEED TO PO-SITION CAROL, DOWN SIX, LEFT THREE. DO YOU COPY? OVER."

Abramson pointed on the map. "It's Con Thien," he said. "We can be there in less than an hour—we'll prob-ably meet some more grunts coming out to help us."

I spoke again into the handset. "Roger, Permission. We copy. Request to know if you've had any other contact with Delta, over."

"NEGATIVE, OVER."

"Roger, out."

Abramson scrambled away and assembled the rest. We gathered at the center of the trail and followed Abramson as he moved into the jungle—away from the firing.

VII. Survivors

We spent three days in the rear, feeling pretty shitty—torn between feeling guilty that we'd run and feeling grateful that we'd survived. We talked it out among ourselves and decided that we'd done the only possible thing. They even called me by name when we talked about it; not Newguy, but Barstow.

At the close of the third day, while we still wondered what would be done with us (they had been pretty hasty about keeping us away from the rest of the troops at Con Thien, and even more hasty about getting us to the rear), I wrote my second letter to mom. I didn't say anything about the ambush, just told her I was back from the field and that I was okay.

But I didn't mail it. I put it under my blanket and decided to wait until morning—mail wouldn't go out until then anyway. I lay on the cot in the darkness, hearing the black guys singing—but it was only in my head. They were as conspicuously absent from the rear as the Armed Forces Radio announcer had been in the field. I didn't know where they were; I just kept trying to hear their together singing, and their blended voices, and their "Teach me hodda Philly Dog," even though I knew the hut they'd been in was empty—a screened, plywood mausoleum.

I felt my foot being shaken. "Barstow," hissed a voice in the semidarkness just before reveille. "Barstow."

Abramson stood at the foot of my cot. "Get up. I got the word." He turned and woke up Jaekel, Kaufmann, and the doc. We all sat up on our cots, yawning and rubbing our eyes.

"I just talked to the night-duty office pinky over at S-1," he whispered. "Got the straight scoop."

That brought us out of any sleepiness we may have felt. At the words "straight scoop" we all sat up and leaned toward Abramson, as if he were some kind of messiah and we were waiting for the words that would save us.

"Company's been disbanded—they were captured."

I felt my jaw drop and hang open like an idiot. But as I looked up, I could see the same expressions on everyone else's face.

"They sent in another company to check the place out. All they could find was a few bodies—but no rifles, no gear, nothin'."

"What happened then?" the doc asked.

Abramson shook his head. "Near's I can figure, they lost comm with the battalion right away. We were the only operating radio, and we couldn't even raise Delta."

"Shit," breathed Kaufmann and Jaekel like twins. And Jaekel piped up, "What's gonna happen t'us?"

"We're transferred—to Recon, just a few huts away. We'll be assigned tomorrow."

"All of us?" asked the doc.

Abramson nodded. "I saw your name on the orders, Doc."

"What for?" I finally asked. "I don't get it."

"Could mean anything," Abramson said, shrugging. "Maybe they don't want it spread around that the gooks captured a whole rifle company—so they just want to bury us in a Recon team. We got a better chance of getting blown away with Recon, y'know," he spat bitterly. "They can't court-martial us—Permission gave us the order to withdraw and head for Con Thien. And if they did try to put us in a court, then they'd have some tall explaining to do about how they lost a whole company. That'd really look good in the *Stars and Stripes*, wouldn't it? Shit, I practically had to drag it out of that office pinky—and he said it'd be his ass if they found out he told me."

"How can they keep that covered up?" I asked. "It'll be

all over the press soon enough anyway—there doesn't have to be any inquiry."

"Uh-uh," the doc said. "All they have to do is say it's propaganda. Communists are supposed to be masters at it. Anything the corps doesn't want to believe is propaganda. Besides, back in the world they're starting to talk about pull-outs. Prisoner returns will follow that. Who's gonna give a rat's ass about a company of grunts when all those POWs come marching home?"

The sun was starting to come up, filtering through the screens and replacing the darkness with alternate light and shadow.

"We should all get the word officially today," Abramson said. "Act surprised when they tell you—geddit?" He looked around at us, and we all nodded as one.

Jaekel turned on his transistor radio and static filled the hut. "Christ," he said, groaning. "Recon." He said the word as if it were really something loathsome like a slug, just before the radio blared with a little pipe tattoo and, "Goooooood *Morn*ing *Viet*-nam!"

We all chorused moans and curses, and Jaekel threw the radio down, smashing it on the wooden floor. "I sweartachrist," he roared. "I'm gonna get t' Saigon one of these days, find out who that fucker is, and I'll ram a radio right up his ass!"

I stood up, stretched, and pulled the letter from beneath my blanket. "Anybody got outgoing mail?" I asked, feeling easy about asking, like I was talking to teammates or a new family. We shared a secret. That made us important to one another. And it made me important in the team—not just a newguy anymore.

They all shook their heads, so I walked out of the hut toward the company office. I noticed that they were already dismantling the insides of it, as if by getting rid of the administration, the company would no longer exist.

I wasn't altogether sure they were wrong.

And if that was the way they wanted it, I'd agree and forget that Delta had ever existed—as far as I was concerned, Abramson, Kaufmann, Jaekel, the doc, and I were the survivors of a mass ambush; and I would play as much a part in covering the capture up as they would.

Even if mom were to ask what happened in one of her letters, I'd tell her whatever the corps wanted me to say.

I pulled out my pen and wrote "free" on the envelope and dropped the letter into the box.

BOOK II
The Walking Wounded

A Shithouse Rat

I finish washing my hands and reach for the handle above me.

It clatters under my fingers, and I hear it clack hollowly inside the tank as the toilet flushes with an empty whoosh. I sit again and stare into the bowl while the water swirls and swirls, disappearing with a strangled glug.

Happens about this time every week—sometimes twice —on Tuesdays and Thursdays. Maybe it has something to do with the Bronze Star. I don't know. I'm used to it, though. After five years I should be.

But it isn't over yet.

Next the remembering will start. That happens every time, too; like a recurring dream, and every bit as vivid.

So I stand up and get a fresh, clean white towel for my hands—I can't have them wet for very long—and I stare into the mirror. I flick the light switch on and off, making myself disappear in a snuff of darkness and then reappear in a blinding-white flash. On-off-on-off-on—my face looking like an old-time movie star's.

The flickering light helps me to remember. If I remember, I will be cleansed and I can sleep. I keep flicking the light switch, and I flush the toilet again. In the intermittent light I watch the water swirl and swirl downward.

A dun-brown pillar of smoke twisted and turned over the rusty barbed wire and ascended into a dusty sky. I watched it rise from the gaseous, flaming pit that bubbled and hissed and popped like a witch's cauldron, then went back to my reading.

It was not napalm from a village-turned-inferno by the ZIPPO tracks that caused the smoke to rise so grotesquely some fifteen meters from where I squatted with my complete Poe. Neither was it a burning tank transformed into a treaded ball of flame by a Viet land mine. Such sights were common in the field, but rare in Phu Bai, the rear area.

It was burning shit.

We had been in the rear for two weeks, resupplying and regrouping after our last operation. Burning shit was a more frequent sight here than burning villages.

The others were returning from their cigarette break. I heard their voices and the scuffling of their boots behind me, carried by the early autumn wind that raised mini-tornadoes of dust to mingle with the smoking shit.

"Whatcha readin' for, Sutherland?" I heard Kaufmann say, sneering. "You ain't in college anymore. If you wuz, you wouldn' be watchin' no burnin' shithole." The other seven guffawed like amused Neanderthals—all except the doc.

They gathered in a semicircle around me: seven other marines and the navy corpsman. We watched the smoke abate as the fire slowly died, leaving a thick, pasty blackness in the pit that glowed like a nearly spent coal fire.

The doc looked over my shoulder. He was always interested in what I read. "What is it today?"

" 'The Purloined Letter.' "

Kaufmann crowed and chuckled. "Purloin—isn't that a kind of steak?"

I never knew why Kaufmann hated my guts. I just supposed that hatred was a way of life with him. He took every possible opportunity to harass me. And along with me he hated all college students, blacks, liberals, Communists, Mexicans, and, of course, Viets.

"Naww—that's 'sirloin.' 'Purloin' is a place in Iowa," snapped Jaekel, one of Kaufmann's squad.

The others joined in the chorus. "That's Des Moines.

86

'Purloin' is where Lance Corporal Sutherland went to college . . . You dumb shit, that's Purdue . . . No, Purdue is someplace in South America . . . Wasn't Purloin a British general in the Revolution?" The laughter continued until the doc told us to cover the pit.

"Okay, let's get on the truck. We just have to do the other side of the base, and we can knock off for the rest of the afternoon."

On the truck we sat and bounced over the rutted road that ran a perimeter around the inside of the base. Huge, rusted, twenty-five gallon buckets rattled and slid around in the back with us. We sat on the edges of the back, keeping our feet up so the buckets wouldn't slam against our shins.

I sat in a corner at the very rear, looking out over the base—a marine shantytown of half-screened huts, made of plywood and galvanized aluminum roofing that made hundreds of mirrors for the sun. Each hut stood in straight rows that only the military seemed able to achieve. Dust clouds swirled in gritty arabesques between the huts and over them, coating the shiny roofs with a dull film.

The truck we rode raised more dust that settled over us all like a screen, turning our olive-drab utilities to a sickly reddish-brown.

It was like this twice a week. Every Tuesday and Thursday the marines in Vietnam dumped their shit. Two men from each squad, one from company headquarters, and me, the platoon radioman, were under the charge of Doc, the company corpsman.

The doc moved toward where I sat. "I've seen you on this detail for the last two weeks. You on somebody's shit list? No pun intended."

"Aww, Doc," Kaufmann piped up. "Don't pay no 'tention t' him. He's crazier 'n a shithouse rat. He volunteers for this detail every goddamned time."

"Jesus," the doc said, wincing at me. "What the hell for? You *like* dumping shit?"

"Course not. But it's better than the rest of the details—raking gravel between the huts, cleaning out the staff and officers' quarters, or digging sod to put around the mess halls for the colonel's beautification program. Besides, I can get the rest of the afternoon off so I can read.

"Figure it out, Doc. It's either work my ass off all day digging sod or dump shit for a few hours and get the rest off."

The doc grinned. "You're a pretty strange person, Sutherland. You read a lot of Poe?"

"Yeah. He writes about guilt a lot. Guilty characters are the most interesting kind. If you like, I'll loan this to you when I'm finished."

"Sure. No offense, Sutherland, but it's rare to find a halfway literate grunt."

I snickered and slipped the book into the left thigh pocket of my utilities and grunted.

The truck rumbled to a halt, and the doc turned toward the rest of the detail. "Okay, Kaufmann and Jaekel, dig the pit over there by the corner of the wire."

The two grabbed shovels and grinned, leaping from the truck, happy with escaping the handling of the shit buckets. The truck drove on.

There were only three shitters on this side of the base. Each shitter was built on a foundation of two-by-fours, about six feet off the ground. On the sides of the screened structures hinged doors of plywood closed over compartments that housed four-handled buckets, exactly like those we carried in the truck.

Each of us brought a bucket from the truck. They were fifty gallon drums cut in half. We pulled the full buckets from the compartments of each shitter, loaded them on the truck, and then placed empty buckets inside the shitters.

The others in the detail chorused their half-snickering gripes: "This is the shits . . . What a bunch of shit . . . This is a real shit detail . . . Man, Sutherland, you sure know your shit."

The stench was overpowering as we got back on the truck. Twelve buckets of shit and piss, replete with flies and making the air an ozone of gaseous nausea. A slight film of dust covered the top of each bucket as the truck drove slowly backward toward Kaufmann and Jaekel. The pit was ready.

I had an odd tendency to be philosophical about this job. Like Hamlet at Yorick's grave, reflecting that everything returns to clay, I considered how everyone is united by shit: the colonel's shit mingled with the corporal's, the provost marshal's with the private's, the chaplain's with the cook's.

And I stared absently into the twelve buckets, reflecting that we rode on a truck that carried three hundred gallons of shit.

In those buckets my own shit mingled with the doc's and with that of the two or three others I could call my friends. Even my enemies were united with me in those buckets—inextricably bound with my shit. I thought about those I despised as I looked into the buckets and tried to imagine whose shit was whose. The oozy, khaki-colored shit would belong to Staff Sergeant Villanueva, who took ecstatic delight in throwing discarded C-rations to Viet kids to watch them fight over food. The hardened globs with flecks of corn and nuts that looked like failed fudge could have come from Pfc Jaekel, who had a fixation for destroying Buddhist temples. The long, tubular shit was probably Private Kaufmann's, he who favored white phosphorus grenades for burning the homes of villagers. The black, tarry shit must have been discharged by Lieutenant Campbell, who enjoyed stuffing hand-illumination grenades in the shirts of NVA prisoners. Here, in a variety as infinite as man himself, was all their shit. And I thought, "Yes. Everything in the Vietnam war boils down to shit."

We emptied all the buckets into the gaping maw of the pit, and the doc poured five gallons of kerosine on top of the oozy surface. He also poured some into the buckets and set them aflame with a match.

I turned to see Staff Sergeant Villanueva drive up in his jeep. He stepped from behind the wheel and straightened himself to a pudgy five-foot-six. His utilities were starched and pressed superbly, and his boots gleamed with a spit

shine like a wine bottle. On his belt, next to his polished
.45 holster, hung two old-style pineapple grenades. The
grenades were polished with Brasso until they appeared as
golden gourds. Villanueva stood and stared at us, as if he
couldn't imagine what we were doing.

The doc looked up to see him and grinned at me.

" 'This is the excellent foppery of the world,' " I said,
laughing, and the doc laughed with me as we watched
Villanueva waddling into the G-5 hut—the civil relations
office.

"What da fuck was dat?" bellowed a pfc in our detail.

"Villanueva," spat out Kaufmann. "Staff NCO of the
PX. That sonofabitch's got more money an' gear than the
whole fuckin' corps."

It was true.

Villanueva made his money off the Viet whores he
brought in for the officers. He made money off the Viet
concession stands that sold Cokes to thirsty marines at a
dollar a bottle—a dollar-fifty with ice. He practically
owned the PX. He sold supplies to the Viets—boots, blank-
ets, even beer. Staff Sergeant Villanueva was a first-rate
civil relations man.

It was a well-known fact that he kept the paperwork on
all his holdings in the black box we could see in the back
of his jeep. It was a sort of mobile file cabinet that he
could take whenever he went to any of his concession
stands or whorehouses.

And it was generally accepted among the lower ranks
that Staff Sergeant Villanueva was a first-rate prick.

The doc went to the truck to get some paper to set the
pit on fire.

Jaekel snickered and elbowed Kaufmann. "Say, I wonder what ol' Villanueva would do if he found his box
missin'?"

A fiendish gleam came to Kaufmann's eyes, and they
both rushed toward the jeep. Jaekel grabbed the box and
Kaufmann helped him carry it to the pit.

Gathering around the yawning, shit-filled hole, the rest
of the detail watched as Kaufmann and Jaekel threw the

box in. It sank slowly, then disappeared with a loud slurp. Until I saw them throw it in, I didn't know what they had in mind. I wouldn't have stopped them anyway, since I wasn't sure what Kaufmann and Jaekel would do. Besides, I had no loyalty to Villanueva.

The doc came back from the truck, rolled up a copy of *Stars and Stripes* into a torch. He dipped the end of the wad into the kerosine, lit it, and threw it into the pit, putting *Stars and Stripes* to its best possible use.

Flames and smoke belched from the pit, and another dun-colored pillar of smoke swirled upward.

I laughed inwardly at the thought of Villanueva's paperwork at the bottom of the six-foot pit, where it belonged. The rest of the detail smiled knowingly at one another as they watched the bubbling, hissing fire turn the surface of the shit to a blackened patina.

"All right, marines," grated a voice from behind us. "Where is it?"

We turned to see Villanueva glaring at us, hands on hips, feet spread, his right hand menacingly near the grip of his .45.

"Where's what, Sergeant?" asked the doc.

"You know what, you squid motherfucker. Who's the ranking marine here? I don't wanna talk to no fuckin' sailor."

"Lance Corporal Sutherland, Sergeant," said Kaufmann.

"All right, Sutherland. Where's my strongbox?"

I looked around at the others, their eyes cast down. Kaufmann and Jaekel looked at me through squinting eyes, challenging me to tell, and threatening me if I did.

"You pukes were the only ones close enough to my jeep. You took it." Villanueva drew his pistol and pointed it in my chest. The fire in the pit burned hot in my face as it grew bigger and I glanced toward it.

Villanueva caught my glance and a slow half smile came to his fighter face. "You two!" he said, pointing to a couple of privates in the detail. "Get a fire extinguisher. Now!"

The two privates ran for the G-5 hut and returned with a CO_2 extinguisher.

"Put out that goddamned fire!"

A private sprayed the pit and in seconds the flames were gone, leaving a thin, white, bubbly foam on the black-coated surface of the pit.

"Now, you're gonna do some diggin', Sutherland. You're gonna pull my strongbox from the bottom of that pit with your hands."

The doc jumped between us. "Sergeant, you can't make . . ."

Villanueva grabbed his shirtfront and threw him to the ground. "I can. Know what disobedience of an order during time of war can get you, boy? The brig officer's a friend of mine, and he can show you a real good time. So you better do it—I'm making that an order."

I gazed into his face, feeling partial contempt and partial disbelief, but saw the twisted, sadistic glee of a tyrant who knows he's in control. Since I'd been in the corps—where every one of your rights as a man are taken away and then returned over a period of years in the form of privileges—I had come to accept humiliation. But I had never imagined anything like this: to grovel through six feet of shit to recover a senior NCO's possessions—if anything, it was too literal. I had crawled through mud to recover the bodies of marines who had been dead and decomposing for days. I had lived with rats in bunkers while being shelled. I had loaded dead NVA on carts to be lined up for body counts. But I never thought it would come to this.

"Do it, Sutherland," Villanueva barked.

I was not about to do time in the brig. It was either dig through this shit or spend years harassed daily by the maniac guards for which the brig was so ominously famous.

I rolled down my sleeves and reached for a nearby pair of gloves.

"No. Barehanded," Villanueva snarled.

I tried to remember where I'd seen the box go down—I might be able to find it quickly and get it over without wallowing for a long time.

Kneeling at the edge of the pit, I looked up at the others.

Some stood mutely gaping like toy-star marionettes. Others stared at the ground. One ran for a nearby hole to puke.

I reached into the pit and felt the warm, oozing mess coat my hands and ran between my fingers. I shuddered at the sensation, and I gagged from the stench of the blackened, kerosine-burned globs.

Flat on my stomach, I sunk my arms in past my elbows and felt a hard, flat surface with my fingertips. Fortunately, the box hadn't sunk to the bottom. I felt around for the edges and grabbed the corners. It took all my strength to pull it up. I held my breath against the smell, but I could hold it no longer and the fumes permeated my every sinus.

The box slipped from my hands as I puked and crawled backward from the pit.

I scarcely heard the explosions over Villanueva's screaming in my ear.

His screams were replaced by cries of "Incoming!" and the shrieks of rocket rounds. I saw the others scatter, running for the nearest bunker.

"Get back in there!" blatted Villanueva, kicking me in the side. I rolled and swung my fist, knocking his pistol into the pit and tackling him with my legs. A roar like two fast freight trains colliding in a tunnel deafened me as I climbed on top of Villanueva and wrapped my caked hands around his neck. He rolled, came on top of me, and I lost my grip. Straddling me, he smashed his fist into my face.

My mouth filled with blood and saliva, and I spit in his face as I saw his fist raised again. His shoulder seemed to explode in a mass of blood and he bleated in agony, his right arm dangling like a crimson rubber snake.

With all my strength I slammed my fist into his balls and rolled him into the pit. I looked around for cover, realizing that I couldn't drag Villanueva with me. He would have to take his chances in the pit.

The rockets still squealed and roared as I crawled toward the shitter. I didn't have time to get to a bunker, and there wasn't room for two in the pit. I hoped I would have enough cover underneath the shitter.

I saw that the Viets were walking their rockets further into the base, and I thought they would walk them out, so I started to run for the G-3 bunker. But I found I was wrong. The cluster of huts that housed G-5, along with Comm and G-2, was ground zero—the Viet's target area. I ran back for the shitter.

Rockets fell in a ghastly, grating rain, obliterating the huts, transforming them into geysers of yellow sparks and shaking the ground like a cataclysmic quake. Smoke and dust and pieces of wood and metal swirled and sang through the air in a hellish tempest. I screamed and screamed to let out my terror and to save my body from the battering concussion.

I watched the explosions, waiting for a break that might give me time to get to a safer position. A ball of flame billowed from the pit, and I saw Villanueva consumed in a vermilion cloud. I heard splats on the plywood sides of the shitter above me, and I saw burning globs dropping on the two-by-fours around me.

The rockets stopped. I could hear no more explosions or freight-train-like whisks. Out of the near silence I heard cries of "Medic!" and names being called and orders shouted.

I felt a hot throbbing on my left thigh and I winced, looking down to see my leg drenched in blood. Reaching into my thigh pocket, I pulled out my complete Poe; the pages were oozy with my own blood, and the shit on my hands mingled with the red smears on the cover.

In a gory heap, Villanueva's body burned half in and half out of the flaming pit. I limped toward him, stuffing my book back into my pocket, and dragged him out. With my shirt I beat out the flames on his torso as I saw the doc and four of the detail coming toward me, followed by Lieutenant Campbell.

"Sutherland! You're hit!" yelled the doc, grabbing me.

"Villanueva, he . . ."

"S'okay, Marine," said the lieutenant. "You did all you could. I saw you trying to pull him out. Doc, take him to sickbay—the rest of you men put out this fire and cover that pit."

I tried to speak. I wanted to tell them what had happened. "Lieutenant, I . . ."

"Don't sweat it, Sutherland. With that leg you'll probably be shipped out early. There'll be a citation in it for you, too."

I looked at the pit, slowly flickering. It flared brightly, then burned low, sending a gnarled, black cylinder of smoke, swirling, swirling, swirling . . .

I flick on the light and leave it shining brightly. My face is flushed and beads of sweat and globular tears make tracks over my cheeks. I taste salt and blood in my mouth.

The water in the toilet bowl is still, and I can only hear the soft rushing of the pipes.

I rush from the bathroom to my bookshelf. Inside my battered and stained complete Poe, the medal flashes its red, white, and blue ribbon in my eyes. The room begins to whirl, and I stumble back to the bathroom, clutching the Bronze Star.

I drop the medal into the toilet.

It clanks on the bottom of the porcelain bowl, and I reach again for the handle. The medal swirls in the water, around and around, until it vanishes with a watery gag.

Yes.

Now, after I dry off with another fresh, clean white towel—yes.

Maybe now I can sleep.

Totenkopf

"Sure, it's genuine," I tell the guy at the other end of the line. "Kaufmann never burns anybody; you just ask any collector."

I twist the phone cord, tangling it in my hand. This guy is beginning to piss me off. If he wasn't offering such a good price, I'd tell him to shove it up his ass.

He's still skeptical—wonders how I get them. "Look, I still got connections. I don't have to be in the Nam to get my goods.

"How soon? I can have it ready for you in about three hours. You come over then, and it'll be waiting for you. If you don't want to buy, you don't have to, okay?

"Yes," I say half-irritated, to let him know where he stands, and that I don't take any shit. "It's still the same price. You know how to get here? Okay—it's the last house at the top of the hill on Bear Creek Road, green with black trim. See ya."

I hang up and go into my workshop—a small room I've built in back of a closet and under the eaves. All my merchandise is in here. Sitting at my desk, I open up my old tin trunk and take out my next sale, polishing it with cotton balls and varnish; thinking that you really have to put up with a lot of petty shit when you're hustling. But it's a good business, always plenty of customers—and it pays the bills, and then some.

Besides, I'm one of a kind—the only Vietnam War souvenir dealer in the country. And all my stuff is top quality because, like I told the guy on the phone, I got my connections.

The shine is starting to come up now from the mahogany stain. If I say so myself, this is a pretty decent piece of work. The bullet hole adds a real authentic touch. This will be worth every cent of the five hundred the guy's going to pay.

I've come a long way in this business—haven't always had it this good. But like everything else, I guess you have to start small.

"Twenty-five bucks," I told the corporal from supply. "That's as low as I can go." He stood there in his starched and pressed jungle utilities and shined boots, his left hand on a sheathed knife at his hip—a knife he'd never used for anything but opening mail.

"Shit, Kaufmann. You can get those gook NCO belt buckles almost anywhere." He started toward the screened door of the hooch, putting on his shades, which looked like two mirrors. "I'm gettin' short—tryin' to save my bread for when I get back to the world."

I looked at Jaekel, my partner in this business and the point man for the team. "You seen any of these here in Phu Bai, Jaekel?"

Jaekel sharpened his knife on a honing stone and shook his shaven head. "Only thing I seen in the rear is beer and typewriters and dry eots," he muttered.

"Besides," I said, waving the buckle in front of the corporal, "you don't know what a bitch it was getting this thing. I had to knife the fucker—couldn't shoot him, he was the advance point of a company. Isn't that right, Jaekel?"

"Christ. You Recon guys sure know how to sling the shit." I saw my reflection in his shades above his smirk.

"Hey, I'm not givin' you no shit—ask anybody in the team. Jaekel was there." I reached under my cot and pulled out my tin trunk. "Okay, look. I'll throw in the gook's collar tabs, too; guess I can afford it." I brought out the red parallelogram collar insignia, with two brass stars on them, and showed them to the corporal. "Well, how 'bout it?"

He nodded. "Okay. Twenty-five," he said, reaching into his pocket, and handed me the money. "When's your next patrol? I got a guy in my section wants some gear."

"Coupla days," I answered, folding the money into my pocket. "What's he want?"

"Pistol."

Jaekel whistled, still sharpening his knife. "That'll be rough. It'd be our asses if we took a weapon and didn't report it."

"Will he pay?" I asked.

"Sure. He hasn't been in the Nam two months yet—just a boot. I'm training him for my job. He'll pay you whatever you want," he said, standing in the door and examining his souvenirs.

I snickered. "Guess those should make for some good stories for the folks back in the world, eh Corporal?"

He looked at us, reflecting us in the mirrors above his stony face, and walked out wordlessly.

I gave half the money to Jaekel, and he sheathed his knife. "Not bad," he grunted. "How much we made off that one gook so far?" He took out some wire cutters and began clipping the tips off his rounds as he took them out of his magazine; then he scored the flattened edges with a hacksaw blade, making dumdums.

"Over a hundred. He was a gold mine, man. Buttons, badges, spare uniforms, collar tabs, and a Sam Browne belt. And the best is yet to come. You been out to the digs yet?"

"Yeah. This morning. That fuckin' Barstow came up while I was there."

Barstow. That boot gung-ho sonofabitch. He'd had a cushy radio job in Lejeune, but he volunteered for the Nam to keep his kid brother out of it—something about the crotch not being able to send two brothers to the Nam at the same time. Now he was our team radioman and a pain in the ass. Always snooping around. "He give you any shit?"

"No," chuckled Jaekel with a toothy grin. "I had it covered back up by the time he got there. The ants've done a great job. A little kerosine and some scraping, and we can deliver tomorrow."

"No shit!" I said, laughing. "Great. That motor-T sergeant's gonna have himself one decent conversation piece."

"Or paperweight."

I rolled back on my cot, holding my sides. "Man, I don't give a shit if he eats out of it—long as he gives us the hundred and fifty."

"He will," Jaekel said, half-smiling, while he clipped the tip off another round.

Near the edge of the perimeter, we dug up the ant hill.

"Hey, you were right, Jaekel," I said exultantly. "Guess the grape jam and sugar really helped. The ants have done most of our job for us. By the way, I forgot to tell you. I got another order from one of the office pinkies yesterday. Should be able to pick one up next patrol—and a pistol if we're lucky."

Jaekel put on his gloves and opened a can of kerosine. "Where's the sandpaper?"

I pulled it from my pocket and tore it in half. We started sanding the skull.

It was about the tenth skull we'd treated and sold, but none before had ever been so clean. Most of the flesh was already gone, and the bone shined white as we sanded off the remaining shreds.

Of all the souvenirs we'd been selling over the past five months, gook skulls brought the highest prices. We sold them to supply, admin., and Comm. Even an occasional Seabee wanted one. And if we didn't make contact with NVA on patrols, it was no sweat to get them off half-dead civilians in some of the villes on the other side of the Z. The assholes in the rear wouldn't know the difference. And if anybody asked questions, we could always blame it on the gooks. We'd only had to take two or three civilian heads to fill our orders so far, but every one of them had brought a good price.

And nobody'd given us any shit about it—except Barstow. The rear-area turds were content to get their goods and rotate back to the States, where they would have their souvenirs to make their war stories believable, even though they'd never come any closer to combat than the editors of *Stars and Stripes*.

We finished cleaning the skull, wrapped it in an empty sandbag, and sat down for a smoke.

"Look, Jaekel," I said, clenching my cigarette between my teeth and cupping my hands around the match to light his. "We got a good thing going here—lotta money, big money. Now, I'm rotating in a month, and you still got four to go, right?"

Jaekel nodded. "Yeah. But I think I'm gonna extend for six months. I'll get a bonus and thirty days leave—probably a promotion, too."

"Okay, what I got in mind is this: We can keep the business going even while I'm back in the world. Back there, guys are making piles off Nazi souvenirs. I should be able to get a market in gook stuff, too—even corner it."

Jaekel blew smoke rings, pulled his knife and began whittling a piece of wood. He answered, grinning, "How do I know you'll send the money if I get the stuff?"

"C'mon man. Kaufmann ever burned you before? It's easy. You just package up the orders I send you, skulls, too. Whatever else you happen to get, sell on your own and keep the bread. But I'll be your clearing house back in the world, and I'll send you fifty percent of the take. I know I can get top prices for stuff back in the world."

"How much you figure for a skull?"

"Well, we'd have to raise the price to cover the mailing charges and the added risk. We couldn't charge the same prices as we do here. I'd say around three hundred."

"Just don't fuck with me, Kaufmann," he replied, glowering at me, and I watched his knife as he whittled the wood to nothing.

"You know I wouldn't do . . ." Someone calling our

names cut me off. I heard it from farther down the wire.

"Pfc Kaufmann, Pfc Jaekel," the voice said, drawing nearer, and we both stood up.

"Shit," Jaekel hissed. "It's that asshole Barstow."

We watched him running toward us, still calling our names—a tall, skinny, baby-faced kid who looked like a recruiting poster even in his utilities.

"Barstow," I sneered as he walked up to us, "we know you're a lance, and we know we're pfc's. So why don't you just call us by our names?"

He didn't pay any attention, just blurted, "Third Team got hit up in the Z—we gotta go and help them get back. Cummon, Lance Corporal Abramson and the doc are waiting." He turned and ran back toward the compound.

"Sombuddy oughta put that little fart out of his misery," growled Jaekel, standing up and grabbing the bag.

"Yeah," I snorted. "Well, maybe we can get a good haul this time, too. Let's go. Y'know, Jaekel—this just might be my last patrol. I'm only three months away from being a civilian."

The chopper dropped the five of us in a clearing and flew off immediately, leaving us in a flurry of flying dust and leaves. We ran straight for the jungle's edge until we could hear the chopper's engines no longer.

Finding a trail, Jaekel took the point—Abramson, Barstow, and Doc behind him, myself at the rear. Moving in a widely spaced column, we made our way toward Third Team's last known position. Every sound—swishing leaves, a cracking vine—caused us to freeze or blend into the thick green of the jungle foliage; the camouflage paint on our faces and the green of our utilities made us vanish as if we'd never been there.

Occasional hisses of static from Barstow's radio were the only sounds we made. "CHECKMATE, CHECKMATE. THIS IS PERMISSION, OVER. REQUEST SITREP, OVER."

Abramson never had to say a word—communicating with us in sign language or shifts of his eyes.

After an hour's march, I saw Jaekel freeze and throw up his arm, signaling a halt. He kneeled down, and I could see him take something from the body of what looked like a gook officer and stuff it in his own shirt. Abramson turned to signal the rest of us to disperse. We melted into the brush and waited in silence, save for Barstow's fast talking into the radio in hoarse whispers.

I grinned to myself. Jaekel must have gotten a pistol off the gook, and Abramson didn't see him take it because he'd turned to signal us. Barstow might have seen it, though—and that might be worse. If he had, I'd have to find a way to shut him up—buy the prick off if necessary.

A snap of Abramson's fingers brought us out to the trail, and we circled up in a clump of brush. I saw Jaekel pat the front of his shirt and wink at me. I knew he had the pistol.

"Okay," Abramson whispered. "Third Team mentioned an ambush. From the looks of this area, this was it, so they shouldn't be far off. I'm going to scout the trail a few meters ahead; the rest of you hang tight here 'til I get back." He left us and duckwalked up the trail.

"Shouldn't you give the pistol to Lance Corporal Abramson?" Barstow whispered to Jaekel.

"Pistol?" the doc said, grinning. "You get a pistol off that gook, Jaekel?"

"What're you talkin' about?" Jaekel grumbled.

"I saw you take it off the gook—you put it . . ."

"Shaddup Barstow!" I hissed.

Abramson crept back into the circle, glaring at us. "What the hell's all this chatter? You fuckers know better'n that!" he growled through clenched teeth. "Now move out, it's clear ahead."

We moved out and passed the wasted gook officer. His face was completely caved in, and his torso was a beehive of bullet holes. I checked him out for gear, but he had nothing we could use—least of all his head.

Another half-hour's march brought us to a clearing where we saw what was left of Third Team.

Five bodies lay grotesquely with frozen stares—mutilated beyond all recognition. Arms and legs lay scattered around the corpses, making the scene look like an exploded department-store window; a couple of their heads were missing; flies buzzed around them by the hundreds, making the humid, putrid air drone with their flight; all their boots, gear, and even their dog tags were gone.

Abramson signaled Jaekel and me to the left flank to clear any possible ambush that might lie there, while he tried to move around to the other side of the clearing. Jaekel and I crawled, five meters apart, through the underbrush, stopping every few meters to look and listen. Reaching the other side of the clearing in the underbrush, we came back to the trail and signaled Abramson, who entered the underbrush we had just cleared and moved toward where we were. Then we began a sweep of the other side of the clearing, crawling, stopping, and listening as before.

Rounds snapped over our heads like loud popcorn, and a machine gun raked the brush atop our heads. I felt bits of branch and leaf dropping down the back of my shirt and hot mud on my face. I could feel the heat of the rounds just inches above my head. I tried to move my body deeper into the ground. Then the firing changed direction—toward the clearing. I heard the doc scream, and I fired toward the machine gun. Barstow was screaming into his radio; I could hear it over the firing—both the screams and the shots seemed to stop at the same time. Jaekel threw two grenades in the direction of the last shots, and the entire jungle seemed to lurch under my stomach. I spit out dirt and tried to clear it from my eyes after the two thunderclaps of Jaekel's grenades subsided, and soon all was silent.

"What'ya think?" gasped Jaekel, crawling next to me.

"I dunno. I don't hear Abramson. He's either dead or bugged out. We better get to that radio."

We crawled to the edge of the clearing. The doc lay tangled with one of the bodies from Third Team. The back of his head was completely shattered, blood and brains around his head like an aura. Barstow lay on his back, covering up the radio, staring straight up—either snuffed or paralyzed, I couldn't tell which. And in this spot, one was the same as the other.

I could hear Permission calling us. Jaekel pulled his knife and crawled toward where the grenades had gone off. I looked down the trail where Abramson should've been and saw nothing.

"Okay, Kaufmann," I heard Jaekel say with a stage whisper, "grenades did the job. Shit, what a mess."

I crawled toward the radio, rolled Barstow off it, and grabbed the handset. "Mayday, Mayday. Permission, this is Checkmate."

"WE ROGER YOU, CHECKMATE," rasped the radio. "WHAT IS YOUR SITUATION AND POSITION? OVER."

"We found Knight's Cross. Completely Cadillac. We've got two Cadillacs ourselves, over."

"WHERE IS CHECKMATE LEADER? OVER."

"Can't find him—we are about a click away from our original LZ."

"KNOW WHERE YOUR PICK-UP POINT IS? OVER."

"S'affirm."

"GET THERE. LEAVE THE CADILLACS. WE'LL GET THEM LATER. DO YOU ROGER?"

"Roger—ferchrissakes hurry up."

Jaekel crawled from the bushes. "Nothin, on 'em we can use. They're just a couple of privates. Heads all shot to shit, too."

"Let's make it to the pick-up point; they're sending a chopper," I told him.

"Wait a minnit. I gottan idea. There's no heads around here we can use," he said, smiling menacingly while looking at Barstow.

"You shittin' me? We don't even know if he's dead. He could just be paralyzed; there's still color in his cheeks, and he's not stiffening up yet."

"Why not? Who's to know?" he snapped. "Heads are money, man. You said it yourself. Big money. There's two hundred bucks waitin' fer us if we get a head for that office fag. That's a hundred apiece! And what the fuck difference it make? When the ants finish, they all look the same—we can blame it on the gooks, just like before. He'd of turned us in for the pistol, you forgettin' that?"

I grinned. "You're a first-class businessman, Jaekel. Just hurry it up. I'm too short for this shit."

"Awright. You take the radio, then we can get goin'—it's like you say, you're gettin' short," he answered, smirking, and pulled his knife.

I finish polishing the skull just as I hear a car door slam outside—then footsteps on the wooden porch.

Going to the door, I see a tall, thin, slightly bearded man in a field jacket and blue jeans. "Mister Kaufmann?" he asks.

"Yes. You the guy who phoned?"

He nods. "Is it ready?"

"Sure. Cummon in. I'll go get it. Have a seat."

I go into my workshop. Putting the skull into a box, I bring it back out and put it on the table. "You look familiar," I say casually. "Were you in the Nam?"

"Yeah," he says, nodding again. "Just got back about a month ago and got out."

"Well, you didn't have the beard then," I said, chuckling. "Still you look . . . What outfit were you with?"

"I was in the grunts."

"Sheeit. That's pretty strange. I mean, I don't get many calls for souvenirs from grunts. It's usually from ex-supply guys or air wing or something. I was with Recon myself."

"I know," he grunts, examining the skull. "Nice piece of work here."

I start to wonder about this guy. How did he know I was Recon? And what does an ex-grunt want with souvenirs? In the year and a half I've been in this business, I've never had any orders to fill for grunts. "How'd you know that?" I ask, dropping my smile.

"I've been checking around. Been wanting to meet you

for a long time now—ever since I talked to your friend, Jaekel."

"Well, I'll be damned," I say, laughing. "You know Jaekel? That sonofabitch. The way he keeps extending, I doubt if he'll ever get back to the world."

"Met him in Phu Bai. He told me you'd give me a good price—he didn't have anything at the time. Three hundred, he said." He emphasizes the "he."

"Well, prices are going up on everything, aren't they? When you see him last?"

"About a month ago. I think he'd be a little pissed if he found out you're only sending him a hundred-fifty for skulls that you're selling at five-hundred."

I don't like this guy. He's getting salty, crowding in on my business. "That's between him and me, isn't it?" I say, putting my hands on my hips.

"Not anymore," the guy says with a slow half smile. "He's dead." He reaches into his pocket, and I hear a loud snick. I see a blade shining in his hand. "By the way, my name's Barstow. I hear you and Jaekel knew my brother," he continues, glowering.

It all makes sense now—why he looked familiar, how he knew so much. This is a set-up. I watch his knife carefully as he continues.

"We thought something was strange when they recovered his body, mutilated like it was. Couldn't even give him a decent funeral. But if the gooks had done it, they'd have taken all his gear, too—all the rest of the bodies were mutilated, sure. But they didn't even have their dog tags, weapons, or anything else. My brother's body did.

"Then I heard that you and Jaekel were in the souvenir business. So I just figured it out from there and went looking for Jaekel whenever I was in Phu Bai. He wasn't hard to find. He helped a bit by telling me where you were, before he died." He picked up the skull and threw it at me. "Shot through the head finished him off; I let him off pretty easy because he was so helpful to me in finding you.

"Now, you might as well tell me, Kaufmann—who did you sell my brother's head to?"

I lunge for him and he slashes my arm and then moves in back of me with the knife to my throat. I force his knife arm down and bend over, throwing him over my back. He flies across the room and slams into a wall.

Running to my workshop, I hear his feet close behind. In my old tin trunk, I see my machete. I unsheath it just as I feel his hot breath on the back of my neck and his blade gouge my shoulder. I elbow him in the balls and he falls backward, then scrambles to his feet.

My arm throbs hotly with its open gash, but I swing the machete in a wide arc, just missing his shoulder and carving off a corner of my desk. He leaps at my stomach, driving his knife into my thigh. I bring up my other knee into his jaw, and he collapses backward over my old tin trunk.

In a short swath I swing the machete in a vicious backhand, and I hear its liquid incision.

His head topples to one side, and a crimson geyser soaks his green field jacket while his body jerks spasmodically and his head rolls to a stop at my feet.

I pick up the head, examining it even as its eyes blink occasionally, and blood flows over my forearm to my elbow.

I catch my breath and say with a snicker to the heap of olive drab and red on the floor, "A little acid, and some steel wool—should draw a good five-fifty."

The Two-hundredth Eye

I. Depth Perception

The blue, gold-lettered sign sticks out of the top of the door frame. I tilt my head to the right and up so I can try to read it as the corpsman wheels me closer to the door.

If I still had both eyes, I could easily read it from down the corridor.

I strain my eye to give the sign depth. I try to contrast its colors on the white wall, but I'm at the wrong angle to see it yet. It still looks like it's pasted on the darkness at the end of the corridor—and even that looks as flat as a photograph.

The corpsman wheels me to the right, in front of the door and below the sign. I can read the golden message now: Lt. Cdr. D. L. Larsen, Psychiatrist.

I hear a buzzer and the corpsman says, "Here we are, Lieutenant. I'll be back to pick you up when the doctor is through. And, Lieutenant Campbell, please don't try and walk back to the ward. I really caught hell for it last time, sir."

As the door opens, I wonder why they don't want me walking by myself. I don't need this wheelchair. I feel like I've recovered.

I am wheeled into a windowless, white room, carpeted in blue. He moves my wheelchair forward and places me in front of a broad, uncluttered, battleship-gray desk with a high-backed, black leather chair behind it. I hear the door close behind me, and I am alone for a while.

Other than the desk and the chair, the room is empty. I am only the third element of the decor. Not that anything else would make any difference—it would just look flat anyway. So I stare at where the white wall meets the blue carpet, creating an illusion that it is the edge of a box pointing toward me.

A highly polished shoe and a starchy white pants leg intrude on the edge of the box.

"What do you see down there?" a voice asks softly as my eye traces up the leg. A shiny belt buckle sits inlaid at the center of a man dressed in milk white. He blends momentarily into the wall. I am drowned in white. Even his hair is white, making his narrow, black-rimmed glasses show up more darkly on his tanned face with the wide chin and wide grin.

"Nothing," I mumbled. "There's nothing down there."

"All right," murmurs the man in white, "look at me."

He slouches in his black leather chair. I hear the starch in his uniform crinkle. "I am Doctor Larsen," he says, placing his hands on top of his head with his elbows pointing out to the sides; in this position he looks like a talking eye. "Can you see me?" he asks, smiling.

"Yes."

"Turn your head to the left. Can you see me now?"

"No."

"How's your eye?"

"Gone."

"Have you looked in any mirrors lately?"

Sure. I've been looking in them since I got to this place. But I don't tell him that. He's a shrink, and that might mean something to him that doesn't mean anything at all. I know how shrinks are.

Sure. I've looked in mirrors. But I'm going to stop because there's nothing in them to see on the right side of my face. So what's the use? It's depressing.

Laren throws a mirror in front of my face. "Then look into this one."

I turn my head to the left so I won't have to see.

"Look!"

II. Mutt and Jeff

The guards threw me into the room and slammed the door behind me. From one window that had glass like a shower door light beamed down and focused on a square, wooden table with two chairs. The room wasn't much bigger than my cell—about six feet on each side—with a cement floor and walls.

It had only been three days since our capture. I remembered scratching a third mark in a corner of my cell with my C-ration opener this morning. The Viets caught my company in a U-shaped ambush and wiped most of us out before they fell on my platoon and the remnants of two others. I counted our numbers while the Viets transported us to where we were—wherever that was.

There were exactly one hundred of us.

I still had a rough time believing it. One hundred marines taken prisoner. That was never supposed to happen. The Code of Conduct said never surrender while still having the means to resist; but by the time the Viets captured us, we were out of rounds and had only knives. Knives do no good against AK-47s.

Sitting in one of the wooden chairs, I waited for whatever would happen. I knew this would be interrogation. They wouldn't bring me down here for anything else—unless it was to kill me.

I hadn't met any of their officers—only guards who looked well equipped and well fed. And I supposed that this would be my first meeting with any officer.

A stream of stereotypes flooded my mind: a Viet officer in a resplendent uniform marching in, laying a pistol on the table, and saying, "You are surprised I speak your language—I attended your Stanford University"; or some huge goon with a rubber hose, slapping it in his hand behind my head while questioning me; or a . . .

The door opened, and the two guards entered and stiffened to attention, bookending a slight, white-haired man with a half smile. He wore khaki pants and shirt with red collar devices. He walked slowly into the room as the guards about-faced and closed the door. Then he moved without looking at me to the other side of the table and sat down, still maintaining his half smile.

"Good morning, Lieutenant Campbell," he said softly. "I am Colonel Tuong of the Army of North Vietnam."

I said nothing.

"Oh, you are going to be silent. I thought for a moment that you were going to tell us everything—pertinent and useless—as many of your men have already done. That would make the situation very difficult. If you had any such information, we would have to arrange for your transportation to Hanoi. And with the volume of bombing attacks we have experienced lately, you would probably be killed by your own B-52s!"

I still said nothing. I knew this game—saying that my men had already informed was an old trick. I would let him do all the talking.

"Very well—Campbell, James D., 074359, Lieutenant, United States Marine Corps; Commander of the Third Platoon, B-Company, First Battalion, Ninth Marine Regiment—I will assume that your silence is due to your own sense of duty and not to any shock at being captured as you were near the Ben Hai River three days ago."

"If you know all this Colonel, why am I here in interrogation?" I answered, smirking at him.

He grinned. "Who told you this was to be interrogation? Like many Americans, you have been shown too many training films. Next, you will be expecting me to strut around the room with a swagger stick and say things like, 'We have ways to make you talk.' Really, I had expected a man of your intelligence . . ." He shook his head and tsked. "I am not a cliché, Lieutenant."

He pulled out a package of Salems from his shirt pocket

and offered me one. "There are many American products I enjoy," he said, noticing my smirk and lighting the cigarette I took from him. "To such an extent that when this foolishness is over, I hope that trade can be effected between your country and mine. And that may not be too long. Your president, I understand, is under a great deal of pressure to bring all of you home."

I inhaled deeply on my cigarette, sending out a long spike of smoke that clouded in the light beam from the window. "I don't know anything about that, Colonel. Now, why don't you tell me where I am?"

He laughed, a high-pitched giggle. "Now you are turning this into an interrogation. Please remember that you are the prisoner."

Still giggling to himself, he stood up. "It would do no good to tell you where you are. You probably couldn't pronounce it anyway, and thus, you would only forget it. You are the senior officer and therefore responsible for your men. Whatever happens, they are your command. Isn't that what your Code of Conduct dictates?"

"When will I see them?"

"I remind you, Lieutenant, you are the prisoner. You are in the Democratic Republic of North Vietnam. You are in this room for—pardon the pun—orientation. Just how long you will be here is uncertain. And that is all I will tell you for the present."

He walked to the door and left the room.

This time it wasn't stereotypes that filled my mind; I knew what to expect next. They'd talked about it in predeployment Code of Conduct classes—the various interrogation techniques used by the enemy. One would play counselor while the other played disciplinarian—the difference between a father confessor and the grand inquisitor. I could tell all my problems to Mutt. I would have them beaten out of me by Jeff.

Tuong had tried to seem too practical, too kind—almost parental with his half smiles and soft tones. The only thing to expect now was a raving, brutal maniac, demanding confessions, screaming abuse, and probably administering beatings.

Tuong had been Mutt. I had yet to meet Jeff.

I sat smoking the cigarette down to the filter before I dropped it on the floor and leaned forward to crush it beneath my boot.

The chair seemed to explode from beneath me. And the instant I hit the floor, I knew I'd been right. I looked up and saw Jeff, one of the tallest Viets I'd ever seen. He stood nearly six-feet-two.

He dragged me to my feet by my shirtfront and sneered down at me at five-feet-ten. He threw me toward the door and out into the corridor. The two guards kicked and prodded me back to my cell. Behind them I could hear Jeff's heavy boots clattering on the cement floor. Face down on my cell floor where the guards threw me, I could still hear them as he walked around me in a circle.

He kicked me in the side. "Get up!"

I came to my hands and knees slowly, and he kicked me again, dragging me to my feet. Bending over, I could see his boots, shiny as a bottle. There were scuff marks on the toes from his kicking me.

"You've ruined my boots!" screamed Jeff. He threw a handkerchief at me. "Wipe them off!"

I looked at him mutely, dazed, my jaw agape. He, too, wore khaki—but it was severely starched and pressed with creases that looked like sword blades. His hair was as black and shiny as his boots and holster, from which he drew a pistol and stuck it in my ear.

"I am Major Hien of the National Liberation Front," he snapped in a clipped accent. "You will do everything I tell you." He pushed my head down, and I sank to my knees. "Polish them!"

I began rubbing the toe of his left boot in small circles until the scuff mark disappeared; then I did the same with the right boot while Hien still held the pistol in my ear.

I tried to keep things straight in my mind—to keep from being panicked. "This is only harassment," I kept telling myself. "It's Tuong they expect me to tell everything to, not this goon. Neither of them had asked any questions, which means one of two things: Either they're trying to scare the hell out of me to make it easier to get information, or they've already decided that I know nothing of value to them, and they want confessions to trumped-up charges."

Hien's boots shone brightly again, and I stopped polishing.

"Get up!" he snarled. "If I have my way, you will all be killed tomorrow, one by one. You will be the last." He stepped back two paces and kicked me in the stomach.

I doubled up on the floor, hearing his heavy boots walk out of the cell, hearing the slam of the cell door. I crawled to my usual corner and passed out.

III. Time Lapse

The cramps in my bowels and bladder woke me up; I had relieved neither since my capture.

Groggily I realized that I was in the opposite corner from where I'd passed out. I knew because I always slept in the corner where I kept my crude calendar. I slept there so I would remember to make another mark on the wall every day.

Moving slowly and painfully toward the other corner, I saw that there were seven marks on the wall. I tried to remember having made the marks, but I was dazed—part by hunger, part by confusion. I kept asking myself if I had made those marks—what had happened? Why did I, how could I, forget four entire days?

I still felt in control of my own mind. The Viets had done nothing yet to make me lose it. I could still remember my name, serial number, hometown, and everything that led up to my capture. So the marks on the wall could have only one explanation: the Viets had put them there.

The door opened. Tuong walked in slowly with his half smile.

"More 'orientation,' Tuong?" I said, sneering at him.

Tuong grinned back and snapped his fingers at the guards who brought in two chairs. "No, Lieutenant. You know orientation ended two days ago as well as I do."

"Bullshit, Tuong. I've been here three days, maybe four at the most."

Tuong laughed his high, shrill staccato bleat which twisted his face and brought out all his wrinkles. "You may believe that if you want. But I assure you, you are wrong. You have been here for a week, even if you don't remember. I can understand how a man in your circumstances could easily . . ."

"Don't give me that, Tuong. I'm not going to argue about how long I've been here. I know I'm right."

"How very American of you," he said, beaming. "I am glad to see it. It would be a terrible inconvenience if you did not think you were still in control of your own mind. You will soon need those excellent mental faculties you possess.

"Now, as to our conversation of three days ago. You will remember that . . ."

"That was yesterday, Tuong."

"I'm sorry, but I must contradict you. Yesterday you were quite cooperative. Three days ago was orientation, and you were very obstinate." He reached into his pocket and pulled out a paper. "Yesterday you signed this. Don't you remember?"

The paper was a "confession" that I was in command of a group of assassins under orders to murder as many North Vietnamese civilians as we could in two days. It further stated that I was an agent of the CIA. My signature was at the bottom.

"Bullshit."

He took the paper back. "Very well. If you are going back on your word, that is of no concern to me. Your signature is here. I must say that you have a tendency to vacillate. Is that an American characteristic? One day you are cooperative, the next resistant."

"Now look, Tuong," I said rising from my chair. The two guards threw me back into it. "I didn't sign anything. I know this is a trick, and I'm on to it. So don't give me any of your . . ."

"Of course. I see this is going to be one of your obstinate days. Very well. I'll leave you now. We'll discuss the matter of your release another time. It is unfortunate that I cannot spend much more time with you."

"Release? What are you talking about?"

"We've already been through this, Lieutenant. I really wish you could remember. I guess your intelligence is not what I thought it was. Alas, first impressions."

"I . . . can't remember."

"So, you now say that you can't remember. A minute ago you insisted that you were right. Which is it?"

"I must have forgotten," I said, still believing that I was right and that four days had not passed without my remembering them. I had to learn what he meant by our release, even if it meant giving in to his way of thinking.

"Good. We'll discuss this another time—shortly. But now we must go our separate ways," Tuong said, beaming indulgently. Then he spoke in Viet to the guards. I only recognized one word he said: "Hien." But when the guards grabbed me, I knew Hien must have gotten his way. "Release" and "separate ways" as Tuong had put it, meant that all of us—one hundred of the men I hadn't seen since our capture—were going to be killed.

The guards dragged me out of the cell. Their obedience to Tuong's terse commands was mechanical—he didn't even have to raise his voice; neither did he have to supervise, for I heard his boots clicking in the opposite direction from the guards and me, down the corridor.

IV. Eyes

I remembered reading that facing imminent death was a sense-heightening experience; one in which we are poignantly aware of life; so that we perceive everything with great scrutiny, so dearly do we want to cling to those last few moments.

But it was not so with me.

My experience did not seem more intense now that I was going to die. The corridor whizzed by me in a blur. The guards might as well have not been there, for I took no notice of them. I had no sudden awareness of all that is alive. No colors were brighter than ever before, no smells more acute, no sensations more real.

I had no sense of inner peace or contentment as the guards brought me out to a sandy, glaringly sunlit yard. I felt no unity with the cosmos as I saw the rest of the captured marines on their knees, their hands tied behind their backs in the blazing sun. And no ultimate love for all that lives overcame me as I saw Hien before my eyes, screaming at me, kicking me, and spitting in my face.

I felt, instead, abject terror at remembering what Hien had said: "You will be the last." I felt disgust that I was to watch ninety-nine marines slaughtered without a fighting chance. And then I was to be killed myself, die helplessly as well.

Hien tied my hands and threw me to my knees in line with the rest of the men. I saw Tuong, standing in the shade of a hut with his distant half smile still on his face, but with a pack on his back. He came toward me, and Hien turned to salute him. I looked around to see that the entire compound was filled with Viets, packed up and looking like they were ready to mount out.

Tuong noticed my scrutinizing his troops. "Yes, Lieutenant. We are leaving. I told you we would be going our separate ways, and we are, in a manner of speaking.

"No, we aren't going to kill you, although it was a valid assumption from your point of view. But we can't take you with us either. Thus, I will leave you in Major Hien's able hands, for the time being. Good-bye, Lieutenant." He turned on his heel and disappeared behind a hut, closely followed by half of the Viet troops.

As if during that time of first waking, when we only hear

unintelligible sounds, I heard a loudening scream to my left. Further down the line of marines I saw two Viets holding down a man while a third gouged out his eyes with a bayonet. They moved down the line, blinding each man as they moved toward me. The screams turned to groans, then rose to screams again with each newly blinded man.

Hien planted himself directly in front of me. "I should think that one eye should be sufficient to lead these others," he said in a menacing, musing tone. "Not one set of eyes, but one eye. You are the leader. Yours will be eye one hundred ninety-nine. Aren't officers ordinarily endowed with more perception than enlisted men? I should not like to break with military tradition."

About fifty of my men were already blinded, screaming and writhing on the sand. Those who still saw cursed, prayed, wept. Terrified and confused, I had nothing more to help me cope than empty memories of the predeployment lectures. I remembered one in particular. "If you are captured, the enemy may force information or confessions from you by having you witness the torture or murder of your men."

It all fit: Tuong's mind games and Hien's brutality. This was another interrogation technique. If it were, it also meant that they weren't really going to release us. In any case, the choice was up to me: Tell Hien whatever it was he wanted to hear, and stop the atrocity; or remain silent and watch ninety-nine marines blinded for life—and that, more than beatings, starvation, even death, I couldn't stand.

"Hien!" I screamed, "I'll tell you anything you want! Just stop it, you sonofabitch, stop it!"

Hien laughed in my face. "Fool. Do you think you have anything we want? You and your herd are a nuisance, an encumbrance. We have to rid ourselves of you, but we can hardly be expected to leave you in any sort of fighting condition."

The guards moved to the man directly in front of me— the ninety-ninth marine. I looked him full in the face, but his face held no expression, only a blank stare with eyes that didn't seem to see me, and then saw nothing at all.

I was beaten, unable to do anything to save my men, not even confess to the Viets. My mind reeled. The sandy yard whirled before my eyes like an obscene carousel. I felt myself wavering on my knees; I retched, my throat burning with the bile and stomach lining that dribbled out my mouth.

I fell to my side, feeling Hien grab my shirtfront and straddle me. I looked up to see him silhouetted in the sun; I saw the bayonet's glinting, and I fainted.

My mouth was full of sand. Fleas crawled on my face and neck. Feeling like I was bound in a cobweb, I awoke to their tickling.

I lay on my left side, my cheek buried in the sand. My hands were no longer tied for I felt the loose cord dangling from my wrist. I wiped the fleas from my face, inadvertently feeling the bloody swelling around my right eye.

I saw only out of the left side of my face. I could see the sand, and the bridge of my nose; it was like looking through a knothole. Slowly sitting up, I saw the rest of the sandy yard come into my half view; the Viets were all gone, and what was left was a gruesome tableau—flat, dimensionless, and, if I hadn't known better, unreal.

The blind lay in line, some groaning, others unconscious and still. Their hands remained tied. I had to turn my head 180 degrees to scan the entire line, for it looked as though some huge partition had been dropped on the right side of everything.

The right side of my face throbbed dully, as if some great bubble of pain were pressing itself further into my right eye. At least the pain was real. It was all that convinced me that I was in no nightmare.

And with that realization I also remembered that I was in command. It was all that kept me from panicking. I might have disregarded all the Code of Conduct dictated up to now, but I could never deny my command. Like it or not, I was a half-blind leader of the blind.

I stood up and surveyed my command: bedraggled, ragged, starved bodies; twisted, dirty, bloodied faces that gazed variously at the sun, the ground, empty space, but saw none. Standing before them, I wondered if I could get them out of this. I even wondered if they wanted to get out.

Not knowing exactly what I would do, I yelled, "Marines! This is Lieutenant Campbell. I can see out of one eye, and I can lead you out of here."

Some moved. Others remained still, staring vacuously away from me. Still others twisted themselves to face me, as if seeking the sight that they knew they would never again have.

"I don't know how far north we are. In fact, I don't even know where we are at all. All I know is which way is south, and that's the way we're going to go."

As I shouted, the pain in my eye throbbed even more and I clutched the right side of my head. "But we've got to work together. One eye might not be enough to get us through; but we've still got our arms and legs. So we can walk back to the south—crawl if necessary.

"You can start by untying each other's hands." I walked to the man on the extreme left and untied him, then turned to the rest. "I want you to count, from left to right. When you hear the man on your left shout his number, shout out yours and remember it. All right," I said, tapping the man with the free hands on his shoulder, "count off!"

The man with the free hands croaked, "One," and the rest followed, "two," "three," "four," with voices that sounded like death groans. At last I heard the final man in the line shout, "ninety-nine."

"Okay—good. Now, all odd numbers turn to the right and feel around until you find the hands of the man in front of you. Untie them, but don't throw the ropes away. Even numbers, when your hands are untied, do the same for the odd numbers."

It took about fifteen minutes to get everyone untied. For many of them, the process was exhausting, and they crumbled to fetal positions on the sand. Another ten minutes and I had everyone with a rope tied on the back of his belt, with each man holding the other end so that the entire line was a sort of chain gang.

They were ready. Getting everyone to his feet required my pulling up those who could not get there themselves. Finally, everyone was standing.

"Hold on to your ropes. Don't tie them to your wrists— if you fall, it'll break your arm. If you lose the rope, yell and we'll stop the column."

I was losing my voice from the yelling, and the pain on the right side of my face was increasing. I looked for water but there was none. The Viets had taken all our gear, including our canteens, so there wouldn't be anything to put water in even if there were any. Neither was there any food. The Viets had left in a hurry, but they had managed to pack all their gear.

Deciding not to tell them of our supply shortage, or even mention it, I moved to the front of the column.

"All right," I called hoarsely to the men, "there's a trail in front of us leading south. We're moving out now. It's just like always, start out on your left foot—forward, march."

They faltered, and I felt a tug at my back. But as I moved forward, I felt the resistance on the back of my belt loosen up. And I looked over my shoulder to see the column moving slowly forward. They staggered and they stumbled, groping with their free hands. But they moved.

V. Bodies

The sun transformed the jungle trail into a steam cooker. Its rays showed as grayish-green beams through the thickness of the jungle canopy. We broiled inside our clothes like so many steaks.

I ached all over. Every joint, with every move; with

every tug of the rope tied to my back, my torso throbbed, a burning sensation that nearly knocked me unconscious.

The men must have felt the same pain, for I heard a chorus of groans behind me; so often that I couldn't distinguish them from my own.

We had marched for three days. Two of the men were already dead, perhaps from hunger—but more likely from despair. I had heard that men in execrable circumstances could and did simply give up, will their own deaths. The two already dead I could hardly blame.

I had thought about it myself, even though I still had partial sight.

I felt the tug at my back again, and my body convulsed in pain. It was a stronger pain this time, and I felt the rope pull me down, then loosen entirely.

Turning, I saw the man behind me curled in a fetal position. His tongue hung out, and he wasn't breathing.

"Halt," I managed to grunt to the column. They accordioned to a stumbling collapse.

I listened to a faint heartbeat, felt a weakening pulse, and watched the third of my troops die. I knew this was also a despair case.

We had no water, but we had sucked moisture from the grass on the humid jungle floor—as most of the men did now, as I did myself. How long we lay there I don't know; each time we stopped seemed longer. And I remembered that with the other two deaths we lay for what seemed—could even have been—hours.

I never told the men about the deaths. If they knew, they never said. In fact we hardly spoke at all throughout the march. I didn't tell them because having to leave the dead behind would have been the final demoralizing effect for most of them. For it was an unwritten pledge among marines that no body would ever be left behind, no matter what had to be done to get it. I had seen these men try for hours to recover bodies that lay decaying in ambush zones, making corpses of themselves as they tried to retrieve the corpses of other men. They could go without food for days, be brutally beaten, cruelly blinded, and broil in a seething jungle as they marched for hours; but they would never be able to stand leaving their dead.

Now, as I coaxed the column to their feet, I broke their pledge for them a third time.

After the fourth day, deeper into the jungle that ran through the center of the demilitarized zone, I knew that most of the men were on the verge of giving up entirely. It took me longer to get them to their feet after stops for rest. I could hear occasional cries of "no," coming from behind me whenever we finally moved out.

For myself, I felt like giving up, too. But what would I do then? Leave these men behind and run off to save myself? I kept going.

What I had dreaded most finally happened on the fifth day.

The shells came one at a time at first. I hardly heard the first two rounds. But the second two came screeching down and exploded in an earthquake of hot breath and flying debris about seventy-five meters to our front.

We fell instinctively to our stomachs, vainly trying to protect ourselves by covering our heads with our hands, restrained and tangled in our ropes as we crawled for cover that wasn't there, venting our primal terror in screams.

I noted somehow that the shells came from the south. They were our own guns, and at this position, they were probably being fired from Gio Linh. I also heard their firing, and it didn't sound far away.

The rounds came in salvos now, and the shattered shells whirled and sang above our heads, tearing away shreds of jungle foliage and peppering us with globs of hot mud. We lay under the fire for—how long? Only those who are not under fire know exactly how long a barrage lasts.

In the silence after the artillery, I checked the column, one by one, to see if there were any casualties. I still had ninety-six men who lay quietly dazed, waiting—I guessed —to die.

"It's over, let's get moving," I said to each one, placing ropes in their hands again.

I would not let them die. I dragged each one to his feet and resumed the march.

VI. Jeff

It was only a few minutes' march until we came to a clearing where the artillery had fallen the most heavily.

The clearing was littered with Viet bodies. They lay in pools of blood; heads shattered, arms and legs missing. Shards of smoldering flesh hung from limbs of trees. Tattered clothing and demolished equipment were scattered about the bodies with grimacing and gaping faces, frozen in their final expressions, blanched and smeared with mud and gore.

I kept the column moving through the newly formed slaughterhouse, picking up canteens and passing them back through the column. We moved forward as we drank, in the direction from which I had heard the gunfire. Where the trail reentered the thick jungle growth, I could see a man lying across it, face down. I bent down to pull him out of the way.

He groaned as I rolled him over. And my eye met the agonized face of Major Hien. His face contorted to a new horror as he recognized me, and I noticed a hole in his side exposing a protruding, punctured lung.

Hien must have known better than to ask for help. There was nothing I could do for him anyway, and even if there were, it was all I could do to keep myself from tearing out his other lung.

I jerked him by his shirtfront to a sitting position, and he shrieked.

"They're all here, Hien. All except three. Look at them, you sonofabitch. They won't see you," I said, hissing. "You've failed, Hien."

He shook his head and gasped for what little breath he

could get. "No. I did not order the blinding. We could not keep you because we were ordered to attack."

He coughed and sputtered blood as I threw him back down. "Tuong," he said, gagging, "it was Tuong who ordered it. And you—you are not . . ."

I kicked him in the side. "Shuddup, Hien. Fuck you, Hien. I only wish these men could watch you rot here. All I want to hear from you is where Tuong is. Tell me, or I swear to God I'll fix it so you die really slow. Where's Tuong?"

"Captured. But I must tell you . . ."

I kicked him again and rolled him off the trail, ordering the column forward. As we marched past the battered body of our former captor, I thought only of Tuong. Tuong. Good old paternalistic, rational Tuong. If I had no other reason to go on now, it was to get Tuong. There would be no more thoughts of giving up now.

With every move of my feet in a slow, half-time step, I could hear his name echoing in my brain.

"Tuong."

I carried on a savage's dialogue in my head, punctuated by the name "Tuong."

"Tuong. I'll get you Tuong. I'll get your eyes Tuong. I'll kill you Tuong. I'll kill you, filthy . . ."

A few hours' more march and we heard the rushing of water. We stood on a riverbank. Here, we would wait.

If that cluster of bodies behind us had been an assault force, a pursuit unit of marines couldn't be far behind.

I lined the men along the riverbank so they could all drink while I watched the other side of the river for troop movement. I kept my head turning to the left and right to scan the opposite bank, for when I looked straight ahead I could see only the left side. My view of the right side was blocked by the bridge of my own nose.

The landscape had no dimension; trees and brush on top of the bank looked awkwardly placed above the river like in a third grader's picture made with paste and construction paper. The river itself sparkled like a lady's sequined evening belt as it flowed under the afternoon brightness. I thought about how much more beautiful it would be if seen with two eyes.

Somehow I couldn't think of myself as being more fortunate than those totally blind men with me. They obviously would never see anything again—ugly or beautiful. But I would forever be tormented with half sight. And was half sight really better than no sight at all?

But I did have one advantage. And it came to me in one syllable.

"Tuong."

I caught a movement on the other side of the river out of the corner of my eye. A group of marines stood, and the group grew in number as they scanned for a fording area. I stood and shouted, tore off my shirt and waved it until I saw one of them point at us.

VII. Eye One Hundred Ninety-nine

Larsen takes away the mirror, and the right side of my face feels numb like I've been to the dentist.

"If your eye is gone," he says, standing up, "where is it? Can't you see it in the mirror?"

I wag my head from side to side. Inside my head, I hear, "Tuong."

"You heard what the specialists said, didn't you?"

"They're wrong. Hien put my eye out. And he put out the eyes of all my men. But we got back. And it was Tuong who . . ."

"Didn't you leave some behind?"

I start to cry. Larsen slaps the right side of my face but I don't feel it because it's still numb.

"You can see, damn you!" Larsen yells. "You only think your eye is gone. The Viets scared you into believing it's gone. It's the penance you have assigned yourself for breaking down and leaving those dead behind and watching the rest of your men blinded. You're the only one who's keeping yourself from seeing."

I rock back and forth in the wheelchair, my arms wrapped around myself. I can feel my mouth open. I look at the floor and the wall junction, and the box corner points at me again.

The door buzzes, and I feel my chair grabbed from behind. I am wheeled around, and I see Larsen and the gray desk and the black chair whirl by, then disappear.

I sit still as the corpsman slowly pushes me down a corridor. Then I turn my head from left to right as we pass rooms with open doors.

In the rooms men lie between white sheets in traction, or with tubes running into their arms and noses, or with oxygen masks over their faces.

We stop, and the corpsman gets a drink of water from a nearby fountain. I look into a room, and I see an old man with white hair. He sees me and tries to sit up.

I think at first that it can't be. But he gives me a half smile—a weak half smile that tells me for sure who it is.

It is Tuong.

Tuong. He has my eye. If I get it from him I won't see halfway anymore. I know he has it because I watch his half smile turn to a scared look from where he lies.

My head reverberates anew with his name. "Tuong. You've got my eye, Tuong."

I jump from the wheelchair, and the corpsman yells at me. I leap on top of Tuong, and I dig my thumbs into his right eye. Tuong screams and tries to fight as I pull his eye from his socket. It dangles from a long cord of muscle and I jerk the cord from the inside of his head. It is slippery with his blood and fluid, but I try to press it into my face as Tuong screams louder and tries to grab it back.

I can feel the corpsman trying to pull me off. He drags at my shoulders, but I elbow him and wrap my hands around Tuong's neck. Pressing, pressing with my thumbs, I can hear him gurgle and I feel his voice box crunch and his body go limp.

I grab my eye, which lies at Tuong's side, and I hold it tight in my hand while three corpsmen pin my arms behind me and wrestle me to my wheelchair. My head throbs, and it feels like pins are going into my right cheek. I feel tears running to the right corner of my mouth.

Suddenly I am dizzy. The corridor has gotten bigger and longer and I feel like I'm higher off the floor. I see Larsen running down the corridor toward me. I can see him with both eyes. He is brilliantly white against a background of deep shadow. I can see beyond him, too.

"He just jumped the prisoner, Doctor. I don't know what the hell's going on. Should we take him up to the security ward?" one of the corpsmen asks.

Larsen looks at Tuong's room, then stands in front of me. "Let him go," he says to the corpsmen.

They loosen my arms, and I hold out my right hand to Larsen.

He looks at the eye, and I smile.

The Diehard

I wake up, and I think I know where I am. But I don't know how I got here; I can't remember anything.

Guys are lying in white beds, wearing blue pajamas, with tubes running out of their arms. One of them looks like a gook, so I reach for my rifle, but it's gone. Besides, I can't move my arms. My helmet and gear are gone too. I can't sit up because my flak jacket's too tight and it's holding my arms in place.

I yell. But none of the blue pajamas moves. As I yell again, two guys come clacking out of a chicken wire and glass cage with a door that buzzes and flashes a red light when it's opened.

The two guys are dressed in white. One is fat with a red beard; the other is skinny and looks like someone in a Schick commercial. Both of them have black eagles with two stripes and a stick with wings and snakes on their sleeves. Their breast pockets are stuffed with pens and thermometer cases. Above the pockets, their names have been stamped under buttons that say, "Welcome Home POWs."

The fat beard's name is Rosen.

The skinny Schick commercial's is Guilder; he tapes gauze over my mouth.

"Orders on this chart here say to take him to psychiatric as soon as he comes to," Rosen says, pointing to a flat table with wheels that flutter as Guilder brings it near my bed-side.

"Super weirdo, huh?" says Guilder, rolling me onto the table.

"Yeh. After the shrink gets done, he'll be off our hands. I've had this kind before—hairy. We'll send him up to Ward Eleven with the rest of them."

"How many are there like him?" Guilder asks as they start wheeling me out of the ward.

"Guy I know up at Oak Knoll said they had twenty-five. There's thirty in this place. God knows how many are still running around over there," Rosen answers, pushing the button that buzzes the door and flashes the red light.

I try to yell. I writhe on the table trying to get up. I can only see the apple-green walls as they go by me backward, hear the wobbling wheels on the table that carries me, smell the disinfectant and alcohol.

I remember a word that echoes in my head. "Check-mate."

I hear it in static as if over a radio. "Checkmate."

I try to yell it. "Checkmate!"

"What's he saying?" Guilder asks.

"I dunno—sounds like 'checkpoint' or something. Marines aren't the most coherent bunch anyway, especially not after they've been running around in the bush for a year like this guy has. They aren't called grunts for noth-ing," Rosen says, snickering.

"Hey, I heard a good one the other day," Guilder says, chuckling. "Know the difference between a fairy tale and a war story?"

"Okay, what?"

"A fairy tale begins, 'Once upon a time,' and a war story begins, 'This is no shit.' "

They laugh and laugh until we get near a main lobby where I see a navy officer's uniform and a bunch of white coats and some business suits gathered around. One of the business suits is saying, ". . . and to show our appreciation for what you experienced in North Vietnam, and for the sacrifices you have made for your country, we, the citizens of San Diego, proudly present you with the keys to this Lincoln Continental, in hopes that . . ."

The business suit fades out and gives way to a tape recorder asking another navy officer's uniform, ". . . tell us, Commander, did you suffer any physical or mental abuse in the hands of the North Vietnamese Communists?"

I twist my head and strain my neck to watch one uniform take the keys and hear the other uniform's answer, which is drowned by applause and the fluttering wheels of the table.

"Sorry, Marine. But there'll be no car keys for you. You should have been captured," says Rosen. "You'll be damned lucky if you ever get out of here to drive."

"What's this guy's name?"

Rosen looks at a metal binder that opens at the top and clatters on the side of the table. "Abramson, John Merritt, 2247815, Corporal. Third Long Range Recon Battalion. MIA since September of '72."

Guilder whistles. "All that time. Christ, no wonder he's so loony."

Abramson.

Abramson.

I start remembering. My name is Abramson.

I remember everything as if in an instant flash as we enter a darkened corridor. I know who I am now.

This is no shit.

I was running. Had been for days, weeks, months—ever since the ambush.

All I could remember was Barstow screaming "Permission, this is Checkmate," into the radio before the gook machine gunner silenced him. I knew I was the only one of five outside the killing zone; I also knew all the rest were dead. That's when I started running.

I had been running all night again. Water from the evening's rain resting on the leaves and branches that I pushed aside spattered on my face, cooling my chapped lips and swollen eyes. Vines tangled in my thickly matted hair and beard.

The sun was coming up on my left, sending strange gray-green rays through the steam. The humidity made my shirt a second skin. I baked inside my flak jacket.

I found a small clearing with some rocks beneath a tree. There was also a hole dug there from someone else's occupation.

I was in luck. The hole had C-rations in it and a bag of half-moldy rice. I threw rocks into the hole to check for traps. It was clear, so I climbed in, taking off my flak jacket and helmet.

The grayish mush that came from the can marked ham and lima beans was filling when mixed with the unmoldy part of the rice.

I cleaned my rifle after I ate and carved another notch on the plastic stock. The notches did not represent kills—they represented days, and I was running out of room for notches.

I counted them carefully—they totaled three hundred seventy-nine; over a year. It didn't seem that long that I had been wandering around in the north.

I had had enough close calls with gook patrols to slow me up. Sometimes I would have to hole up in one spot for weeks while they occupied the area as a base camp. Getting chow was no sweat then. I could either steal it from their supply area or find one stray NVA to kill, take his rations, and hide his body. But my progress toward the south was slow. And I had long since decided against surrender.

I finished cleaning my rifle and curled up in the hole, pulling leaves and brush over the top for concealment. As I dozed off, my mind echoed, tormenting me as it had so often done since I had begun running with, "Checkmate... Checkmate," and the screams of the helplessly dying.

I awoke to a rushing, swishing sound; like steam pouring out of a boiling kettle. I thought it was the wind, but there were no leaves moving. Except for the continual swish, swash, everything was silent. I came from my hole, rifle first, seeing that the sun was to my right now, and about an hour or so from setting behind the jagged peaks of the Laotian border. It sent orange rays through the jungle steam. I collected the remaining food and moved away carefully from the hole.

I made my way toward where the noise seemed to be coming from. It grew louder—and I knew then that it was the rushing of water. Fifty meters more, and I came to it. I threw my helmet into the air and laughed as I found myself on a riverbank.

If I had been moving south—and I had been, marking the sun's position carefully every day—this river had to be the Ben Hai. It ran through the middle of the demilitarized zone. Cross it, and go about five thousand meters, and I would be in the south. I searched for a fording area, and sat down to wait for nightfall—it would be a safer crossing then.

There were enough rocks in the shallow point to make the crossing easy. I got to the southern bank and started running again. I couldn't stop now, not until I could tie up with American forces.

I knew that a system of four bases called Leatherneck Square lay about two thousand meters to the south of the Z. All I had to do was to get to one of those bases, and I'd be home free.

I kept running.

Con Thien seemed like it would be about the easiest of the four to reach. The base would be occupied by marines. I could pick up a chopper there that would take me to some base further south. Then I could hook up with another unit and get back to finishing this job.

My tour was long past over, but I had made up my mind to extend it. A job is a job.

Orders said never to surrender.

Orders said to keep at a job until it was finished.

Orders said never to run.

I had already broken one of those commands; I swore I would never break another. I had to see this through. And I would.

I came out of the jungle to a cleared area. I knew it was the anti-infiltration strip that had been carved across the country in '67. It ran from Gio Linh on the east, to Con Thien on the west. In the darkness I could barely see the faint outlines of bunkers against the night sky.

There was a house to my left, just inside the jungle's edge. A ladder on the ground would give me entrance to the loft window where I could keep watch. I approached carefully, raised the ladder, and climbed inside.

I took off my flak jacket and lay on it as if it were a mattress, and I used my helmet as a pillow. I lay waiting for the sun. Deciding that there wasn't really any need to keep watch, I fell into dreams unlike those I had had in the entire year's running. There were steaks, glasses of wine, cold beers, and stunningly beautiful women, all before me, inches from my grasp. I was restrained by I didn't know what; on a treadmill that got me no closer to the people and the things I had not known for over a year.

A clanking of mechanized vehicles awakened me. Choppers thwapped overhead. I rose and looked out the window.

I felt my jaw drop and my face freeze.

There was no Con Thien. What I had thought were bunkers were the frames of houses, half-completed. What I had thought were tanks were bulldozers. And where I had expected to see marines, I saw gooks; some dressed in olive drab, others in khaki, still others in black, most in motley.

I squatted at the window in confusion. I knew I was in the right place. Had to be. I had crossed the Ben Hai, followed the anti-infiltration strip, and moved along the DMZ. This *had* to be the south.

So what the hell were all these gooks doing here? Were they northerners? Southerners? Where were the Americans?

I cursed myself for being such a dumbass and working myself into this trap. Now I would have to work my way out—shoot my way out if necessary. I could hole up in the area until they left, which I had done often enough before.

But where would I go? And if I tried to leave at night, which direction would I take? And there was no telling how long they'd be here.

It only occurred to me then, that I hadn't heard any shooting. I couldn't remember the last time I'd heard any fire at all, except for the B-52 raids along the Laotian border. I had always sort of taken noise for granted, assuming that it was part of the environment, and would therefore always be there.

It could be that a cease-fire had been called, and the gooks were taking advantage of it by building up this area. But how did they get control of Con Thien in the first place? And how could they build openly without fear of an air attack?

I heard a creaking behind me, and I turned my head to see a man on a ladder leading from the floor below. He peered over the top of the trap door.

I whirled and fired.

He dropped to the floor, and I jumped from the window and ran for a nearby tree line; it was the only thing in sight that could give me any cover or concealment.

I found some rocks under a bush and checked my ammunition, expecting a standoff: six magazines at twenty rounds each, five hand grenades, and one survival knife. I couldn't hold out long, but I might be able to raise enough hell to draw any American forces in the area to the scene —if there were any. If there had been a cease-fire, they might have drawn back; but the cease-fire was broken now, and that was sure to draw somebody's attention.

I saw a jeep approaching, driven by the same guy I'd shot at in the house. He stopped and pulled a bull horn from the back seat.

"Marine," he droned from one hundred meters away, "come out, the war . . ."

I didn't let him finish. I fired an automatic burst at him, and he dived to the ground with shards of his windshield scattering around him. That was twice I'd missed the sonofabitch. If he gave me another chance, he'd be dead.

It wasn't uncommon for gooks to speak English. They

had warned us about that in the predeployment lectures back in the States. All he wanted to do was to get me to surrender. I wasn't going to, not now, not ever.

The jeep drove slowly out of the area, back toward the house. He was driving on his belly.

I would have to wait for night to move out again. This was another jam I'd worked myself into. I had run for the first available concealment, not bothering to notice that the tree line was isolated in the middle of an open area, with nothing but a long stretch of bare terrain between the jungle and me.

The bulldozers stopped moving and sputtered to a halt. I saw the gooks scurrying away from them and out of sight. I waited.

I heard choppers again. They droned across the open field and landed amid a flurry of gravel and sand. In the dusty clouds, I could see armed, olive-drab troops jumping from the doors of the dragonflylike troop carriers. They formed on line and began moving my way.

I heard a salvo of rounds pop and hiss above my head, and I fired back, moving my position about fifteen meters with every series of five shots.

I dropped to my stomach after my third movement, and the ground shook with an explosion. I hugged the earth, feeling like I was going to fall off. I choked, saw a white cloud of gas surrounding me and blinding me to the advancing gooks. Where had they gotten the choppers? Where had they come from so fast? Where were the American troops—even the ARVN? I gagged, rolled on the ground, choking, curling up. I drew my knife, waiting for the first one who came close enough. I heard their voices, a few meters away. I gagged again, and everything disappeared within the white.

Then I neither heard, nor smelled, nor saw anything. I could only sense my own screams.

"Ferchrissakes, Abramson, shuddup," says Rosen as he pushes another button outside another door. The door slides open on both sides as a red sign comes on that says, "Enter."

"What's he screaming about?" Guilder asks, pulling one end of the table through the door into a white room where the fluorescent lights blind me because I'm staring at them on the ceiling.

"Who the hell knows? You'd be screaming, too, if you'd been running around in the jungle for a year or so, scared shitless of being captured, or being bombed by your own planes; then to find out that the war you'd been fighting has been over with for months."

"How'd they find him?"

"Report says that ARVN picked him up outside Con Thien. He thought they were all NVA, stood 'em off in a fire fight before they had to gas him. It's like I said, you'd be screaming, too."

"It's hard to imagine. I mean, how could anyone believe the war's still going on over there?"

"Use a little imagination, Guilder. They found Japanese soldiers on islands in the Pacific up to twenty-nine years after the Big Two ended. Besides, this guy was long-range Recon. He could've been as far north as Hanoi for all we know. How would he know the war's over?"

I scream, "No!" It isn't over. I bite at the gauze, struggle on the table.

They've captured me. They're Russian advisors—that's why there's no gooks here. They're trying to brainwash me. That's how I forgot my name. That's how I got in this place with the guys in blue pajamas and tubes in their arms. It's all set up. They're doing this to extract phony confessions just like the indoctrination lectures said.

Rosen opens a door. I see a sign sticking out of the top of it: Lt. Cdr. D. L. Larsen, Psychiatrist.

I am wheeled in. I smell pipe tobacco mingled with coffee and Aqua-Velva.

"Here's the latest MIA, Doctor," says Rosen.

"What's that tape doing on his mouth? Get it off," orders the doctor. Guilder takes it off, and the doctor waves them both out.

The doctor sits down. I hear his heavily starched white uniform crinkle. I see his starched smile as he lights his pipe and sticks it in his face.

"You're safe now," he says, smiling. "Do you know where you are?"

I look at him from where I lie on the wheeled table. I see him sideways. I say nothing.

"You're in San Diego Naval Hospital. The war is over—for you, and for everyone."

I try to get up from the table. I have to run. This is no doctor; he's a Russian interrogator. They told us about this one, too. They take one, maybe two guys, to treat you shitty, then one comes along who treats you real good—gives you cigarettes, talks about your girl—to get you to sign phony confessions, get all the information they can.

I know this game. I don't say anything. Not even my name.

"Checkmate" vibrates in my brain, but I don't say that either.

Nothing.

"Do you believe that you are safe here? I can't help you unless you do believe it. Neither can I help you unless you talk."

He's lying—he wants me to talk so he can find my weaknesses—this isn't San Diego—the war isn't over—if it was, I wouldn't be in their hands—this is a stage—everything is—everything—the hospital, the uniforms, the business suits, the Continental—indoctrination lectures said there's no lengths they won't go to to get information and confessions—and if the war was over, I'd know it, and even if it is, we won.

And that's no shit.

VIETNAM

NOVELS WRITTEN BY
MEN WHO WERE THERE

THE BIG V William Pelfrey   67074-7/$2.95
"An excellent novel...Mr. Pelfrey, who spent a year as an infantryman in Vietnam, recreates that experience with an intimacy that makes the difference."
The New York Times Book Review

WAR GAMES James Park Sloan   67835-7/$2.95
Amidst the fierce madness in Vietnam, a young man searches for the inspiration to write the "definitive war novel." "May become the new *Catch 22*." *Library Journal*

AMERICAN BOYS Steven Phillip Smith   67934-5/$3.50
Four boys come to Vietnam for separate reasons, but each must come to terms with what men are and what it takes to face dying. "The best novel I've come across on the war in Vietnam."
Norman Mailer

BARKING DEER Jonathan Rubin   68437-3/$3.50
A team of twelve men is sent to a Montagnard village in the central highlands where the innocent tribesmen become victims of their would-be defenders. "Powerful." *The New York Times Book Review*

COOKS AND BAKERS Robert A. Anderson   87429-6/$2.95
A young marine lieutenant arrives just when the Vietnam War is at its height and becomes caught up in the personal struggle between the courage needed for killing and the shame of killing. An Avon Original. "A tough-minded unblinking report from hell." *Penthouse*

A FEW GOOD MEN Tom Suddick   87270-6/$2.95
Seven marines in a reconnaissance unit tell their individual stories in a novel that strips away the illusions of heroism in a savage and insane war. An Avon Original. "The brutal power of defined anger." *Publishers Weekly*

AVON Paperbacks

VIETNAM

On Sale August 1984
DISPATCHES Michael Herr   68833-6/$3.95
Months on national hardcover and paperback bestseller lists.
Michael Herr's nonfiction account of his years spent under
fire with the front-line troops in Vietnam.
"The best book I have ever read about war in our time."
                                         John le Carré
"I believe it may be the best personal journal about war,
any war, that any writer has ever accomplished."
                    Robert Stone (DOG SOLDIERS) *Chicago Tribune*

On Sale September 1984
FOREVER SAD THE HEARTS Patricia L. Walsh   88518-2/$3.95
A "moving and explicit" *(Washington Post)* novel of a young
American nurse, at a civilian hospital in Vietnam, who worked with
a small group of dedicated doctors and nurses against desperate
odds to save men, women and children.
"It's a truly wonderful book...I will be thinking about it and
feeling things from it for a long time." Sally Field

On Sale October 1984
NO BUGLES, NO DRUMS Charles Durden   69260-0/$3.50
The irony of guarding a pig farm outside Da Nang—The Sing My
Swine Project—supplies the backdrop for a blackly humorous
account of disillusionment, cynicism and coping with survival.
"The funniest, ghastliest military scenes put to paper since
Joseph Heller wrote CATCH-22" *Newsweek*
"From out of Vietnam, a novel with echoes of Mailer, Jones and
Heller." *Houston Chronicle*

AVON Paperbacks

WORLD WAR II
Edwin P. Hoyt

THE MEN OF GAMBIER BAY   55806-8/$2.95

Based on actual logs and interviews with surviving crew members, this is a powerful account of battle and desperate survival at sea, the story of the only U.S. aircraft carrier to be sunk by naval gunfire in World War II.

STORM OVER THE GILBERTS: 63651-4/$2.95
War in the Central Pacific: 1943

The dramatic reconstruction of the bloody battle over the Japanese-held Gilbert Islands which the U.S. won after a week of heavy fighting that sustained more casualties than the battle of Guadalcanal.

TO THE MARIANAS: 65829-9/$3.50
War in the Central Pacific: 1944

The Allies push toward Tokyo in America's first great amphibious operation of World War II, the drive northward through the Pacific to capture the Japanese strongholds on the Marshall and Mariana Islands.

CLOSING THE CIRCLE: 67983-8/$3.50
War in the Pacific: 1945

Drawn from official American and Japanese sources, is a behind-the-scenes look at the military and political moves that brought the Japanese to final surrender in the last sixty days of action in the Pacific.

ALL BOOKS ILLUSTRATED
WITH MAPS AND ACTION PHOTOGRAPHS!

AVON PAPERBACKS